The Rose Garden

READING MARCEL PROUST

Kristjana Gunnars

RED DEER COLLEGE PRESS

The Publishers
Red Deer College Press
56 Avenue & 32 Street Box 5005
Red Deer Alberta Canada T4N 5H5

Acknowledgments
Cover design by Susan Lee
Text design by Dennis Johnson
Printed and bound in Canada by Quality Color Press for Red Deer
College Press

5 4 3 2 1

Financial support provided by the Alberta Foundation for the Arts, a
beneficiary of the Lottery Fund of the Government of Alberta, and by
the Canada Council, the Department of Canadian Heritage and Red
Deer College.

COMMITTED TO THE DEVELOPMENT OF CULTURE AND THE ARTS

Canadian Cataloguing in Publication Data
Gunnars, Kristjana, 1948–
The rose garden
ISBN 0-88995-150-0
I. Title.
PS8563.U574R67   1996   C813'.54   C96-910309-3
PR9199.3.G793R67   1996

Author's Acknowledgements

I wish to thank the German Academic Exchange Program for making my stay in Germany possible. I also thank Dr. Prof. Herbert Zirker of the University of Trier, Germany, for instigating the invitation and for his kind assistance while I was there.

. . . and more than once, as I was reading, it brought to me the scent of a rose which the breeze entering through the open window had spread through the upper room. . . .

— MARCEL PROUST, *"On Reading"* (54)

THE ONLY THING I truly remember from my sojourn in Germany during the summer of 1992 was a garden out back. It was a small garden comprised of a tiny lawn, a small cement patio, and a bed for trees and bushes round the corners. Along one side were a few rose bushes. The street behind the garden was one level up, and the houses on that street looked straight down into my garden. I trained myself to ignore the lack of privacy. I had a project for the afternoons while the sun shone. It was to read Proust's *Remembrance of Things Past*. All the while I had the scent of the pink roses and the vague recall of their continuous presence.

5

Now, I thought, I will not read Proust in an orderly way. I will dip into those three volumes at random like you would dip a poisoned pen. Am I a hostile reader? Or simply a perverse reader? Would Proust have approved of the way I lived with his spirit, even when I was not reading? Even when I was working inside on the dining table in the mornings? Putting notes together on Mavis Gallant? Or at night, reading *The Paris Notebooks* and straining to decode what people were saying on German television? Or in the middle of the day, plowing through shelves at the university library, trying to find out what the Germans were doing with Canadian literature? All that time, dragging Proust around?

Perhaps I was a perverse reader. It was a perverse summer. I had these beautiful hours of solitude with thoughtful texts, yet in the backdrop a crazy drama was going on. The presence of a lover I was working hard to repel. He showed up, we had heated arguments, he left again noisily late at night. Everyone on that street could hear exactly when he came and when he left. All I wanted was to be left alone with meditative texts. Perverse because I refused whatever came easily. I was living in a land full of meat, and I ate no meat. It was the Mosey Valley, flushed with wine, and I drank no wine.

❧

I often went to the railway station in the town of Trier, where I was living. Not because I was always going somewhere. Only on occasion did I visit other towns and countries by train. The rest of the time I was driven madly on the Autobahn by the man with whom I argued incessantly. As the discussion heated up, the speedometer arrow rose to frightening numbers.

I visited the railway station because of the trains. The railway station had a strange sense about it, which reminded me of my life. That the reason why I disliked spending the summer in Trier was not because the place was not pleasant, the people accommodating, and everything to my liking. It was because I had no daily life. My state of mind resembled the atmosphere of the train station.

Unhappily, said Proust, *those marvellous places, railway stations, from which one sets out for a remote destination, are tragic places also, for if in them the miracle is accomplished whereby scenes which hitherto have had no existence save in our minds are about to become the scenes among which we shall be living, for that very reason we must, as we emerge from the waiting-room,* abandon any thought of presently finding ourselves once more in the familiar room which but a moment ago still housed us. We must lay aside all hope of going home to sleep in our own bed . . . (1:694).

The railway station as *mise en scène.* An unpredictable production.

In "The Umbilicus of Limbo" (1925), Antonin Artaud says, *By your iniquitous law you place in the hands of persons in whom I have no confidence whatsoever . . .* [doctors, druggists, judges, midwives] *. . . the authority over my anguish . . .* (70–71). That you have authority over yourself only within certain parameters. Once the intensity of your emotional life becomes too great, you are given over to so-called "experts." "Expert" is simply a euphemism for "owner."

I was thinking of Artaud because of the graffiti. Someone went about the town painting curious sayings on walls, stone fences, bus shelters, and on the railway station. They were political statements belonging to no group. Just an individual venting her anguish on the facades of the town. Because she did that, it was understood that she now belonged to the legal system, once they were able to find her. Artaud, it seemed to me, simply wanted some opium to fight off what he termed a "disease" *called Anguish* (70).

Just because his writing appears on white paper instead of urban murals does not mean Artaud is not a graffitist. His sentences are graffitilike. They smash at you like angry spray paint. Statements like: *All writing is garbage* (85). Or: *The whole literary scene is a pigpen, especially today* (85).

Artaud is also the one who wrote, *I have only one occupation left: to remake myself* (84).

This must be why Proust is so captivating. He knows what he is thinking. He does not dispel your thoughts or blow your thoughts apart, like Artaud. Proust gathers your thoughts together. You calm down. You can sense how one sentence follows another, without strain, without difficulty. Without anguish. Proust is not ragged and frayed and spastic like Artaud. Even though the raggedness of Artaud is powerful, the tranquil rose garden where I found myself reading Proust was more captivating.

Aimé exuded not only a modest distinction but, quite unconsciously of course, that air of romance (II:168). "That air of romance." That soft scent in the air. You know it is there, yet you do not notice. A perfume that melds into the air you breathe. You forget it comes from the fragile petals of those flowers on their thorny stalks.

That cohesiveness that says to you the world is a safe place is also the power of romance. Romance is the backside of anguish.

It is, for example, possible to have an agonizing drive from Trier, Germany, to Strasbourg, France, wherein you think any minute you will become roadkill. You argue all the way over things like "commitment" without knowing what that is, your lover wanting you to "commit" something you do not have: to him. Then, to have a romantic weekend in Strasbourg. You forgot everything that was said. What did you say?

We were walking hand in hand along the river canal in Strasbourg. It was the dark of night. The last revelers had left the crooked streets of the old town. Lights had been turned off. The water in the canal did not move. Suddenly, unaccountably, I had an idea that we would be surrounded by rats. Then I noticed there were no stairs up to the street. We had become lost in a labyrinth of love talk. Just by a slight turn of the head I noticed my entrapment.

On the other side, speaking of "the mystical rose," Julia Kristeva says some curious things about Nerval, "the Disinherited Poet." *The "flower" can be interpreted*, she writes, *as being the flower into which the melancholy Narcissus was changed . . .* (154). The Narcissus flower. I cannot help but think of a book by Linda Hutcheon: *Narcissistic Narratives.* Is it because he reflected too much, or because he was too melancholy, that Narcissus became a flower? Kristeva quotes Nerval: *"An answer is heard in a soft foreign tongue"* (154)

. . . at the same time as it invokes the memory of those who will love the writer ("Forget me not!") (154). I find these thoughts of hers curious and disjointed. And yet. The "answer" that is "heard in a soft foreign tongue"— Can the answer be understood? Does the narrator understand the "foreign tongue" that whispers back to the melancholy spirit in the garden?

The television was in German; the grocery clerks were in German; the bus driver was in German; the typewriter saleswoman was in German. I thought I understood German, but it is possible I misunderstood German instead. It was not German that spoke in a "soft foreign tongue."

Also, when you speak of "the memory of those who will love," you are collapsing past and future. It would be a *Remembrance of Things to Come.* This is possible, especially when speaking of love. Love, unlike melancholia, collapses all things together. Melancholia holds all things apart, at a distance. So it is the lover who speaks back to the writer and promises not to forget.

The objects that induced in me the greatest depression were the shutters in my house in Trier. You pushed a button in the wall next to the window and dark brown wooden panels slid down, covering the window and shutting in place. When the shutters were down, it was dark as a tomb in the house. Not a fleck, string, crack of light got in.

Those shutters are my *Madeleines.* They depress me whenever I think of them. I can hear those mahogany panels slide down along the windowsill, a deep humming sound with a snap at the end just as the last flecks of daylight vanish. Those sticks of wood came down like bars on a prison cell.

Proust's Cottard says, *"The Princess must be on the train. . . ." And he led us all off in search of Princess Sherbatoff. He found her in the corner of an empty compartment, reading the* Revue Des Deux Mondes. *She had long ago, from fear of rebuffs, acquired the habit of keeping her place, or remaining in her corner, in life as in trains, and of not offering her hand until the other person had greeted her. She went on reading as the faithful trouped into her carriage* (II:921).

The Princess has learned, "from fear of rebuffs," to "keep her place." To "remain in her corner." I draw the conclusion that only a few moments earlier, Marcel Proust could not decide whether the Princess Sherbatoff was a refined lady of noble birth or the keeper of a brothel.

The conclusion Proust draws is that *Big restaurants, casinos, local trains, are all family portrait galleries of these social enigmas* (II:922). On trains, at casinos, in restaurants, class distinctions are erased. All is theater. You cannot decide whether she is a lady or a whore, a scholar or a Madame. There is nothing she can say or do to convince you either way, so she simply keeps on reading.

The suggestions Julia Kristeva draws up in *Black Sun*, "The Life and Death of Speech," are instructive. She speaks of life lived as an experience of *separation without resolution, or unavoidable shocks, or again pursuits without result* (36). Mundane reality offers no solutions: *the child can find a fighting or fleeing solution in psychic representation and in language* (36). An alternative to language is *inactivity, or playing dead* (36). Life, as she formulates it, is a *melancholy dilemma*, a condition of *learned helplessness* (36). *The child* [the adult] *needs a solid implication in the symbolic and imaginary code* (36).

Given the "melancholy dilemma," we resort to language. To the symbolic order. People who are depressed, further, do not have this recourse. For the depressed person, language is dead. The symbolic order fails.

For this reason, I was interested in the Trier graffitist. One day a group of professors and lecturers from the university took me to a wine cellar to try the first results of an experiment with Mosel red wine. Since it was a white wine kingdom, producing red wine was nearly irreverent. As we sat around the table, my companions told me the Trier graffitist was actually a woman of about eighty. This information surprised me, for some of her writing was located in places one would have to be an acrobat to reach. Such as the walking bridge over the highway by the campus.

Still, I thought this woman may be mad, but not depressed. She acted out her condition in language. Could this also be said of the Princess Sherbatoff in Proust's local train? In her "learned helplessness," she keeps reading?

Or, for that matter, Antonin Artaud, who speaks of *the terrible inertia of real thought, after verbal memory and vocabulary have disappeared* (189).

Of *the mind living amid the collapse of language . . .* (189).

There is also the factor of Catholicism. Unlike most other German towns, the majority of Trierites are Catholics. Trier is the oldest German town. It has Roman ruins. At one time the townspeople voted to be part of France, but they became part of Prussia anyway. This is something they never quite got over.

I never got over the Catholicism of Trier either. When I was given the keys to my townhouse overlooking the vineyards in the narrow valley below, I opened the door and walked into a Catholic tomb. I was rendered speechless and could never explain to my hosts what the problem was. The problem was that in every room were icons of saints staring down at me: from windows, from walls, even from the backs of doors when I closed them. And the walls of the building were so thick you could scream your loudest and no one would hear.

There were also the shutters.

I took refuge in the rose garden because it was outside the reign of the accusing eyes of St. Boniface, St. Paul, the Mother Mary. Those saints gave me the impression I was doing something wrong. I was not supposed to be there.

There was more to this, of course, than simply the icons in my home. It was one reason why I was uncomfortable in Trier: It was impossible to be there and remain innocent. Even if you bother no one and stay home enclosed in your garden, you are doing something wrong. Perhaps it is just the ambiance of the region. Something I had forgotten. Something we have to read Kafka to be reminded of.

It occurred to me that Northrop Frye addressed this in a mythological context in *The Great Code*. Frye writes that the Biblical Job *wishes, like the hero of Kafka's* Trial, *which reads like a kind of "midrash" on the Book of Job, that his accuser would identify himself, so that Job would at least know the case against him* (195).

Better yet, *He wishes for his accuser to write a book . . .* (195). By extension, the book that K's accuser has to write is *The History of the World* (Frye 195).

What was true so long ago must be true today. If something was true at any time, can it cease to be true later? Or perhaps any truth is a form of art. In "Within a Budding Grove," Marcel Proust asserts *that there can be no progress, no discovery in art, but only in the sciences, and that each artist starting afresh on an individual effort cannot be either helped or hindered therein by the efforts of any other* (1:896).

At the same time, as Northrop Frye notices, details of literature *begin to come loose from their moorings* (217). *Epigrammatic comments,* he writes, have been taken out of the literary texts of their origins and copied and memorized out of context (217). It is as if a given text displays itself as an encasement of useful comments one may remove at random. *What is happening here,* Frye explains, *is that the work of literature is acquiring the existential quality of entering into one's life and becoming a personal possession* (217).

Perhaps I am not a perverse reader, but a possessive one. I am possessive of the text because I know no one can improve on Proust. Not even Marcel Proust can improve on Marcel Proust.

As to reader aesthetics, a student of mine recently told me he read my book on acid. On acid it was a "great book." Then he read it again straight, and it was "so different."

No matter how far from it we have come, the situation of the reader is explained as exactly as possible by Stanley Fish in *Doing What Comes Naturally* when he talks about modernist aesthetics. What is the reader supposed to do? Given the controversy over interrogation, does the reader interrogate the text, or is it the text that does this to the reader? How do you establish an interpretive community? To Fish, *the rule is that a critic must learn to read in a way that* multiplies *crises, and must never give a remedy in the sense of a single and unequivocal answer to the question* (137).

In other words, there never is an actual answer to the question of the text. There is no single purpose or meaning. In that sense, the reader should act as terrorist. Should blow things apart. The ideal reader for Marcel Proust, it seems to follow, would have to be Antonin Artaud.

A good reader destroys the work read in such a way that it cannot be reassembled. In "An End to Masterpieces," Artaud has this to say about the matter: *We must put an end to this idea of masterpieces reserved for a so-called elite* (252). What is the point of a great work? *The masterpieces of the past are rood for the past* (252).

I wonder at Artaud's hostility, his sense that great books are just tombs. No spirit sits up wakefully in them. As to reading, *Let us leave textual criticism to academic drudges and formal criticism to aesthetes, and recognize that what has been said need not be said again; that an expression does not work twice, does not live twice; that all words, once uttered, are dead and are effective only at the moment when they are uttered* (253).

Is it not remarkable, though? How Proust

lived his life once, then again when he wrote it, then again when it is read, then again every time it is read. Because he follows each moment into its core. When Marcel is a young boy he longs for the good-night kiss of his mother, and he is anguished that she leaves again so soon. The reader anticipates and sorrows prematurely with him because *the moment in which I heard her climb the stairs, and then caught the sound of her garden dress of blue muslin, from which hung little tassels of plaited straw, rustling along the double-doored corridor, was for me a moment of the utmost pain; for it heralded the moment which was bound to follow it, when she would have left me and gone downstairs again* (1:13).

At least it seems so to me. Even though all the characters in the scene are gone—the boy, the mother, the guests downstairs have all gone home— somehow their shadow lingers. Here in the boy's text, penned much later in adulthood. A memory even then. An illusion by then, perhaps. I have here the shadow of an illusion at best, dead words at worst.

I suddenly wish to accuse Artaud. The crime is to think in terms of endings. As if anything, whether real or illusory, could actually die. That life occurs only in fleeting moments. I want to return to

Northrop Frye because somehow looking at the Bible as another text, just another text, appears illustrative. Frye talks about the word *beginning:* It is the first word in the Bible. That Frye accuses Christianity of *tenaciously clinging to the notion of the finite and gaining little by that emphasis* (108).

But Frye qualifies what is meant by "beginning," and by extension, by life and death: *We get a little closer to this question when we realize that the central metaphor underlying "beginning" is not really birth at all. It is rather the moment of waking from sleep, when one world disappears and another comes into being* (108).

So Artaud's dead text is only a sleeping text. The sleeping beauty.

But here is the centerpiece of my existence in Trier: that too many thoughts, memories, emotions were triggered simultaneously at every moment. I could hardly look at the vineyards outside, at the stone ruin that once served as a wine press, at the leaden sky hanging over the valley with drops falling, at the facades of ancient buildings in the town center,

22

without innumerable sensations over which I had no control.

For this reason, the little garden out back with the roses provided me with a setting for sorting out some of my impressions. That I had Proust's great work in my lap as I soaked in the sun was incidental, but incidentally I noticed Marcel Proust had come into the same enigma. He had trouble reading the newspapers because words printed on the newsprint caused too many associations, words like *le Secret, Good Friday, Calvus Mons* caused in him a *violent shock. Some moments after the shock, my intelligence, which like the sound of thunder travels less rapidly, produced the reason for it* (III:553).

At least the thunder of Proust's intelligence traveled faster than mine. I could not discover the reasons for my strong impressions. Proust's explanation for these feelings seemed to me very clear: *After a certain age our memories are so intertwined with one another that what we are thinking of, the book we are reading, scarcely matters any more. We have put something of ourselves everywhere, everything is fertile, everything is dangerous* (III:553–554).

To find yourself in everything, to find all things are fertile with you, must be the reflection that lay in Narcissus' pool. The reason for his melancholia. That the more deeply you read into a book, the more it is your book. That somehow I myself have been scattered all over Germany, and it was the shock of my own discovery that led me to this rose garden. Because I recognized, without any certain recognition that "everything is dangerous."

If it is not here already, here in Proust's *Remembrance,* the move to anti-narrative is not far away. There is a sense in which the reader is burdened by historicity, which makes accusations as it progresses. The progress of history. I am trying to keep in mind accusations leveled at Proust and other early twenti-eth-century avant-garde writers like Joyce and Musil: that they gave rise to the *neo*avant-garde, to Robbe-Grillet and Beckett. Instead of the *nouveau roman,* we get the *nouveau nouveau roman.* As Linda Hutcheon explains it, the practitioners of the *nouveau nouveau roman, these poets-turned-novelists saw political implications in their denunciation of the traditional bourgeois normality which formed the optic of the "old" neorealistic novel.* What constitut-ed the syntax of rebellion and progress at once *became the declaiming of "fluent lies"* (130–131).

"Fluent lies" such as the ones Proust told. In fact, any fluent narrative presents itself as a lie. Fluency cannot be true. Was it Proust's mistake to think he was writing representationally, instead of simply creating his own heterocosm?

What is the reader to make of the presence of historicity looming all around? In the church towers that ring on Sundays. In the graffiti on the wall of the cemetery that says, *The Pope is an enslaver of Women!* Written by some eighty-year-old woman at night when the town is asleep.

Linda Hutcheon tries to address the position of the reader in relation to what she calls "self-conscious narratives": narratives that reflect on themselves (unduly, like Narcissus). She writes, *When a person opens any novel, this very act suddenly plunges him into a narrative situation in which he must take part. . . . Overtly narcissistic texts make this act a self-conscious one, integrating the reader* (139). The text has sucked you in, absorbed you. At this moment you are lost in the labyrinth of a "novelistic code." However, *In covertly narcissistic texts the teaching is done by disruption and discontinuity, by disturbing the comfortable habits of the actual act of reading* (139). For this reason, I am *absorbed* in Proust: I find myself in a rose garden,

faintly conscious of the scent of pink roses nearby.
But I am *jarred* by Artaud. I do not know exactly
where I am located when I read Artaud. I have a vague
recall of the core of an American city, where stray
dogs wander with tongues hanging out amid tin cans
rolling on the pavement and homeless squatters in a
bus shelter, wrapped in dirty blankets.

But Hutcheon says more: *The unsettled reader is*
forced to scrutinize his concepts of art as well as his life values.
Often he must revise his understanding of what he reads so fre-
quently that he comes to question the very possibility of under-
standing. In doing so he might be freed from enslavement not only
to the empirical, but also to his own set patterns of thought and
imagination (139).

They said of John Milton that his writing
was so dense it was impossible to understand. They
said only Milton could understand Milton. I do not
care, actually, whether I understand Milton or not. I
do not care whether I have understood Marcel Proust.
If my *mis*understanding is good, why should anyone
care? Even if my misunderstanding has no value.
Appropriate understanding is beside the point. So is
the fluency of the lie.

I can see through the window, looking in, that the shutters have not been driven all the way up. A few of the panels cover the top part of the window, shielding the room inside from the starkest sunbeams. Instead, the rays fall heavily on the Persian carpet. I am reminded of those empirical shutters, half closed, half open.

But here I must stop myself. Just as Linda Hutcheon thinks—inevitably?—of the reader as *he*, does it matter that the reader is *she?* What happens to the text when *she* reads it? Does she, as well, "question" her "understanding"? I am drawn to the argument of Hélène Cixous and Catherine Clément in *The Newly Born Woman: And if we consult literary history, it is the same story. It all comes back to man—to his torment, his desire to be (at) the origin* (65). *Now*, they write, *it has become rather urgent to question this solidarity . . . bringing to light the fate dealt to woman, her burial—to threaten the stability of the masculine structure that passed itself off as eternal–natural, by conjuring up from femininity the reflections and hypotheses that are necessarily ruinous for the stronghold still in possession of authority* (65).

What would happen, they ask, *to logocentrism, to the great philosophical systems, to the order of the world in general if the rock upon which they founded this church should crumble?* (65) What indeed?

What happens to *The Great Code* when she, the woman, sits down in her rose garden to read a book? Can she be an innocent reader? Is the act of reading itself not suspect if she is the reader? If she is the one who gazes, not the one gazed at? The code that, in Frye's words, says, *if the monster that swallows us is metaphorically death, then the hero who comes to deliver us from the body of this death . . . has to be absorbed in the world of death—that is, he has to die* (192). A code that says, in effect, *the Deluge has never receded, and we still live in a submarine world of reality* (192). Someone must pull us out of the dark canals.

But Cixous and Clément have another reading: *So all the history, all the stories would be there to retell differently; the future would be incalculable; the historic forces would and will change hands and change body—another thought which is yet unthinkable—will transform the functioning of all society* (65).

Strangely enough, the mythology changes as

they speak: from fish to vermin. *We are living in an age where the conceptual foundation of an ancient culture is in the process of being undermined by millions of a species of mole (Topoi, ground mines) never known before* (65).

Imagine that. Millions of moles. That is, once the reading women open their eyes, *When they wake up from among the dead, from among words, from among laws* (65). Sleeping beauties all. Sleeping in the woods in glass coffins. But wait. *Most women who have awakened remember having slept, having been put to sleep* (66).

It occurred to me, therefore, that I was getting a little closer to the reason for feeling so suspicious. So under suspicion. So under the watchful eyes of the Saints and neighbors. Under scrutiny, it seemed, by all of Germany. Because the watchful eyes were my own. As I had scattered myself over everything, I looked back at myself from everywhere. But the wonder of it was that, in looking, my eyes had to be open. It followed, my eyes were open. Everything appeared to me to be dangerous because, in this position, in the position of the reader, everything is dangerous.

I began to see women readers gnawing away at the foundations of an old order. But they looked so serene. They really did. Deceptively serene. Sometimes in the afternoon, I walked down to the museum. The museum was located in a bright new white building set in a landscaped park. A rectangular pond with water fountain lay in middle, and walkways around it, adorned with tulips, roses, linden trees. There was a café on the verandah overlooking the park. There I sometimes saw a woman reading, a coffee on the garden table, a swan on the water, a slight breath of wind rustling the crowns of the trees above.

Similarly, the code she, the woman reading in the park, is reading against, can be blacker still. "The monster that swallows us" is perhaps "metaphorically death," but also the so-called Western Code itself. The code that is also present in "alternate mythologies" of the West, as George Steiner outlines them in *Nostalgia for the Absolute*. Steiner writes that after the decline of the great religion(s), other mythologies have taken over: Marxism, Freudian psychoanalysis, and Lévi-Straussian anthropology. All of these "mythologies" swallow themselves. In "The Last Garden," Steiner talks about the vision, the rage, of Lévi Strauss: *The fall of man did not, at one stroke, eradicate all the vestiges of the*

Garden of Eden. Great spaces of primeval nature and of animal
life did persist. The eighteenth century travellers succumbed to a
kind of premeditated illusion when they thought to have found
innocent races of men in the paradise of the South Seas or in the
great forests of the New World. But their idealizations had a cer-
tain validity. Having existed, as it were, outside history, having
abided by primordial social and mental usages, possessing a pro-
found intimacy with plant and with animal, primitive man did
embody a more natural condition. . . . Coming upon these shadows
of the remnants of Eden, Western man set out to destroy them. He
slaughtered countless guiltless peoples. He clawed down the forests,
he charred the savannah. Then his fury of waste turned on the
animal species. One after another of these was hounded into
extinction or into the factitious survival of the zoo (31–32).

An elaborate mythology, simplistic and melo-
dramatic at best. Inspired by great—personal?—guilt.
Feelings of guilt. Self-accusation. But within this
framework, if the innocents in the last garden exist
"outside history," why not say the woman reading is
also an innocent in the garden? Can she be? Does
innocence preclude the act of reading?

But these great, totalizing, mythological con-
structs are phenomenally depressing. They act like
those shutters on the German windows: they come

down and shut everything off. Shut you out or lock you in. There is no escape.

But then I think: It is only language. In actuality, in separation from phenomenal experience, Lévi Strauss has spoken of something that does not exist. Or that only exists nominally. I am trapped in his language, and it encloses because it is unexamined. Heidegger remarks in *On the Way to Language* that *The word alone gives being to the thing* (62). The world does not exist for us outside of language. This can work in reverse. Language alone can give rise to worlds we cannot experience. Fantastic worlds. Imaginative things. The boundary between reality and language continues to blur. *This is why we consider it advisable,* Heidegger writes, *"to prepare for a possibility of undergoing an experience with language"* (62). It will become clearer that when we speak, we conjure. And unless we speak, unless we name the thing we see, it will not be noticed.

Unless I say there is a woman reading in the park, she is not there. I must also tell you what she is reading. She is reading *Remembrance of Things Past* by Marcel Proust. She is thinking that Proust conjured himself through this text. Brought himself into being because he named his own life, he existed. He exists, in other words, because he is read. It is not an existence in itself, rather a life lived in the reader.

Let us for once refrain from hurried thinking, Heidegger suggests. Let us be still and allow the scent of roses to penetrate. It is a vague scent, only noticeable after you have been in its presence for a while.

In "The Fugitive," Proust discovers the world-creation of a word. He is speaking with Saint-Loup about Albertine. Saint-Loup tells him that in order to visit Albertine, he had to go *through a sort of shed,* and into the house where *at the end of a long passage* [he] *was shown into a drawing-room* (III:480). It is a harmless description of the geography of a house. But Proust has never seen the house that Albertine is staying in. He is shocked by the realization that it is a real house with real rooms.

At these words, he writes, *shed, passage, drawing-room, and before he had even finished uttering them, my heart was shattered more instantaneously than by an electric current, for the force that circles the earth most times in a second is not electricity but pain. How I repeated to myself these words* (III:480). It is the words themselves that give him pain. More pain, perhaps, than he would have felt going there himself. The pain of discovering a person who is the object of your imagination also has a phenomenal existence. That existence is proven. There is a witness. Someone who can verify there is a shed, a passage, and a draw-ing-room in Albertine's house. *In a shed one girl can hide with another, he reflects. And in that drawing-room, who knew what Albertine did when her aunt was not there* (III:480). And now he must imagine the possibility that Albertine could have a secret life of her own. That she, the object of his imagination, could have an imagination of her own. He is shocked: *those words uttered by her concierge had marked in my heart as upon a map the place where I must suffer* (III:481).

The pain inflicted by language: an operation through the surface into a depth we do not under-stand. The surface of language. The possibility that the surface is all. That the mind is a flat plain without depth. All of psychology would be an illusion. The unconscious, the subconscious: an illusion. Imagine, writes Fredric Jameson in *Postmodernism, Surrealism without the Unconscious* when describing "the newer painting," *in which the most uncontrolled kinds of figuration emerge with a depthlessness that is not even hallucinatory* (174). Imagine *Chagall's folk iconography without Judaism or the peasants, Klee's stick drawings without his peculiar personal project, schizophrenic art without schizophrenia, "surrealism" without its manifesto or its avant-garde* (174–175).

What Albertine may be doing when her aunt is not there. Creating figurations unconnected to anything. Albertine herself may be a figuration without connection. The pain that there may, in actuality, be no connection between Albertine and the one who feels pain at the thought of her in a drawing-room, where no one can see her. No one is watching. She is uncontrolled. She is disconnected. Imagine, on the other side, Albertine without Albertine. It will be pain felt over nothing. The shock of discovering the object of your pain does not exist. You feel pain for no reason. Just because the electric shock you experience is evoked by language alone.

We were walking through a narrow alleyway

in Strasbourg. It was the middle of the afternoon. A
dry haze appeared to penetrate the air, but it also
seemed the haze was not there. It was Sunday. The old
town was deserted at the peripheries and congested in
the center. Where we walked, there were no people.
Shop doors were closed. No one's image appeared in
any windows. Perhaps everyone was asleep. Taking
siestas in midafternoon. We had become lazy. Holding
hands lazily, even our talk of love had become lazy.
Talk of love was a pleasant diversion suddenly, instead
of an intense invitation to self-apprehension. We were
privately, each on our own, impressed by the thought
that we were talking about something we did not
know existed. How do people "love"? How can you
say you "love" someone when tomorrow it may not be
true? That "love" is a figuration brought about by
nothing, by haze in the air. Romantic love is perhaps,
at best, what Anthony Burgess in an essay called "Creativity" calls *an arabesque of smoke from an expensive cigar*
(Mariani 269).

The man with whom I often argued, frequently laughed, and now was pointless and lazy with,
who was my lover then. We came away from Germany
because there was not enough of the *carnivalesque* in
our lives there. He was a diplomat: for him Germany

was all diplomacy. For me Germany was all serious study. It was tomes of books in libraries. It was the faintly musty halls of great men of the past. Men in frocks. Men with large collars and long hair. It was a private house overlooking an old vineyard that enclosed me like a tomb. Thick walls and dense shutters and interior darkness.

Our steps became slower and slower. We could hear a fly buzz. A bicycle bump over some cobblestones. A geranium stood crooked in a window terrace. We were conscious of how lovers pain one another. The possibility that we have inflicted pain on each other because we are lovers. That is what lovers do.

Suddenly, the narrow alley opened into the city center. Sunday excursionists were crowded into the small square. Eating ice cream. Sitting on terrace café chairs with beer on the tables. Dominating the square was a carousel: beautiful wooden horses that sailed up and down, in circles to tinny music. As if in calling a truce to an eternal warfare, we went on the carousel. Sitting on the wooden horse, holding the pole with my left hand, I found it suddenly absurd: going around in circles in Strasbourg, seeing buildings

designed aslant and pointed into street corners sail by
as they might in a strange dream. He was on another
horse lower down: when I looked down he was laughing. I was laughing. It was the laughter of being
caught in the charms of a disengaged language.

But how the love life, the life of the emotions
of love, has been conveyed by those conscious of their
feelings, able to articulate them. The disconnectedness
that is conveyed there: Proust, who speaks of her
when she is not there. Sören Kierkegaard, who speaks
of her when he does not know her. Kierkegaard's narrator in *Either/Or* stands by a house on the Strand,
waiting for an unknown woman to reappear. He
knows her name is Cordelia. He sees a resemblance
between his Cordelia and King Lear's Cordelia: *that
remarkable girl whose heart did not dwell upon her lips, whose lips
were silent when her heart was full* (277). The beauty of
Cordelia is that she does not speak. She does not tell
her love: Like the Princess Sherbatoff, reading in the
railway carriage, who has learned to "keep her place,"
Cordelia is silent.

That I am really in love, Kierkegaard's narrator

says, *I can tell among other things by the secrecy, almost even to myself, with which I treat this matter. All love is secretive, even faithless love when it has the necessary aesthetic element* (277). He knows the verity of his own feelings by his reluctance to articulate them. The more he speaks of his feelings, the less real they will be. Love will be spent in the speaking. Transferred out of the nervous system into language, where it will exist in a disembodied form.

But perhaps his trepidation results from the opposite: what he fears is the possibility of bringing his feelings to life by naming them. In language there is self-invention. The fear of creating a relationship where there was none before. Of making a fleeting, evanescent relationship, which like all human affairs drifts in the smoke of time, permanent. By writing something you make it eternal.

Over and over again I discover the diary is an effort against loss, Anaïs Nin writes in her journals of 1944–47; *the passing, the deaths, the uprootings, the witherings, the unrealities. I feel that when I enclose something, I save it. It is alive here. When anyone left, I felt I retained his presence in these pages* (4:142).

An attempt to possess, to hold onto, what must necessarily be taken away from you.

For that reason, articulated by a woman, I bought a typewriter in Trier. A simple, white typewriter, which I put on the heavy table in the dining room. I found hidden in a bureau drawer a colorful cloth which I draped over the table. When it rained, I kept the door to the little garden open. From the table where I worked I could hear the heavy drops fall on the porch and leaves. Sometimes I wrote a page: anything that came to mind. I could not understand my own feelings. Perhaps by writing them on the white typewriter, something would be clear to me. I did not want to lose my thoughts. They must be trapped in the net of words.

Or perhaps it was something else still: the fear of being rooted in the suburban feeling my neighborhood induced in me. I felt as though I had lived in this heavy house for decades. I was familiar with the routes the children took to school. With the way the neighbors came in and out of houses at regular times. The weekly garbage truck. The daily mail. The bus heading up and down the avenue: I knew when it went up, when down. The expectation of a note on my door from a neighbor: "Your porchlight was on all night."

I did not want to become part of the plan of this old town. Part of its human geography. I wanted the air: the roses: the rain. In her 1944–47 journals, written during the war, Anaïs Nin one time exclaims: *The conflict in my life is the conflict in my novels: opposition of an ugly reality to a marvelous intuition or dream of other worlds. Not permitting the human to destroy illusion. Opposing the artist to the world of authority, power, and destructiveness* (4:105).

Because a woman can be trapped in a system that denies her. She must always remember the "marvelous intuition." She reads not because she wishes to, but because she has to. It is necessary. She either reads or dies.

Through no effort of my own, I stumbled upon a medieval town in the vineyards north of Trier. Somehow I arrived there by bus and got off near the entrance of an ancient monastery. The town was maintained in its original style. No innovations or developments were to interfere with the stucco houses, gabled and beamed wood, or the crooked cobblestone lanes that passed for streets. Roads were too narrow for cars, so people had to leave them outside the town gate.

It was a custom of mine not to memorize any names. I do not remember the name of that town. I did not want to move as a tourist. I was not a tourist. I lived there. I did not carry a map or a dictionary or a notebook or a camera. Like all the other people living in the area, I had come to Bilbert on a Sunday, dressed in Sunday clothes, to saunter through the medieval lanes. No one was in a hurry that day. We all walked slowly and greeted each other politely when we passed. I have christened the town Bilbert: we were all having a Sunday outing in Bilbert.

I was thinking of the Sunday outings with the family in Denmark, where I lived as a child. When Danish life was still genteel and people went in small groups with wicker baskets to the park. We took wicker baskets with bread and apples to the park and watched the deer among the trees. We sat on blankets on the ground and spread plates and utensils, cutting board and wine bottle, on a table cloth. Everyone was lazy in those days. They drank wine and became more lazy.

It was in Bilbert I found myself standing in the book room of the old monastery. It was an abandoned monastery, now used as a residence for the oldest people of the town. The complex still had a study room and book room. They were large, high-ceilinged, stuccoed rooms with deep-set latticed windows overlooking a sunny courtyard. Vines grew about the windows, and trellises stood up along the walls. Inside hung oil-painted portraits of men in deep red frocks, some with pointed hats, others with flat ones. These men were readers. Then they were writers of what they read.

It was also that time I thought of what Jean Cocteau once said. In his *Diary of an Unknown*, he reflects that *all of this would be funny if it weren't sad. One gets the distinct feeling that the more man learns, the more he seeks and believes himself to have attained the mystery, the further away he drifts, for he is down a long slope of errors that he has no choice but to follow, though he supposes himself to be climbing up it* (76).

I was looking into the courtyard: so quiet and serene, where one could walk in large circles among flowers and greens, meditating without distraction. I was thinking if it is a slope of errors, what an attractive slope it can be.

On the bizarre and beautiful carousel in Strasbourg's town square, I was on a higher horse than my lover. When I looked down at him on the outside ring, laughing, I saw he was happy. He was not always happy. For the most part he was frustrated, upset, unhappy that I would not acquiesce to a perfect relationship. It occurred to me that I would not yield because I did not want him to be happy. Because I did not love him. It was too simple to be acceptable to him. Like many lovers, he created complicated reasons for our malcontent.

To accept that someone does not love you is complicated. Experience teaches everyone those labyrinths. Some, like Marcel Proust, can articulate them. *When I was in love with Albertine,* he writes, *I had realised very clearly that she did not love me* (III:939). Such a simple statement to make, yet it will not come out.

We will say almost anything else: because to claim you are not loved is too final in a world where closures never seem to occur. All endings are temporary, tentative. With a turn of the head, we extract new meaning, better meaning, out of such disappointment. Meanings like: she is too involved in her books. She should read less. She is dragging around *Remembrance of Things Past* to the detriment of real life. Things present. For Proust, however, there is a minor heroism to looking into the face of people's emotions: *I had had to resign myself to the thought that through her I could gain nothing more than the experience of what it is to suffer and to love, and even, at the beginning to be happy* (III:939).

I know I am a fickle unfaithful reader. I take Albertine's part and reject the voice of the narrator. I understand why Albertine might not love the narrator, Marcel. My reading poisons the well of Proust's sincerity. He did not count on the unpredictable reader. And I am not unaware of the danger I am in. If I persist in this demeanor, the demeanor of the one who does not love and yield, I will eventually be rendered invisible and thrown away. Because at the moment, there is no other world.

As soon as we try to reflect on the matter, Martin Heidegger writes, *we have already committed ourselves to a long path of thought. At this point, we shall succeed only in taking just a few steps* (101). Small steps to an unknown destination. You do not know where this thinking will take you. Or when you have gone wrong. Everything you say turns out to be something else. It becomes necessary to follow the logic of a line of thinking, regardless of your fading love for the thought. You no longer care for your argument, yet you must make it, for you are committed to it. There is a love affair between you and your argument.

Perhaps this is why I am able to read Proust and remain in the neighborhood of his thinking the way I can remain within the perfume of the rose garden. Because the scent is gone when the wind changes; then it is back. Subtle, barely noticeable, it is a poetry of breathing. And Proust himself wafts his thoughts, so nothing quite sticks. There is always another angle. Proust, it appears, is a fickle unfaithful writer. He will not be loyal to single thoughts, but allows them all to operate at once. Or to disappear if it seems better to be gone.

As a matter of fact, Heidegger himself admits that *Thinking is not a means to gain knowledge. Thinking cuts furrows into the soil of Being* (70). It has not become necessary to reflect seriously on the subject after all. The only requirement made of the reader is that she allow herself to remain in the neighborhood. To be there and notice the peculiar fragrance.

Is it, then, that literature takes over from life? That reading and its consequence, writing, take away from Being? And love: can love only occur at the expense of literature? On the 27th of July 1867, Gustave Flaubert wrote to George Sand, *I was not so 'submerged' in work as not to want to see you. I have already made enough sacrifices to literature, without adding this one* (81). To sacrifice yourself, as though on an altar, to a certain deity. How can literature have such power? Yet it does. That the writer is always unfaithful to the lover: because literature is a greater love, more demanding. The writer's lover is always jealous.

Or is it, rather, as Antonin Artaud supposes, a war between life and death? That written texts are not life? But something else. *We must put an end to this superstition of texts and of written poetry,* he writes in his essay "An End to Masterpieces." *Written poetry is valuable once, and after that it should be destroyed* (255). What is that once, when a text is valuable? Is it to the writer of the text, at the moment of writing? Can there be any value for the reader? *Enough of personal poems which benefit those who write them much more than those who read them,* he says (256).

Artaud's answer to the malaise of the written text, which intervenes in the act of living, is simple. He writes, *This is why I propose a theater of cruelty* (256). To merge literature into life, so what we have is theater. And in this arena, there is cruelty: *a theater that is difficult and cruel first of all for myself,* he adds (256). So it is not a matter of a writer falling into Narcissus' pool, but of the writer participating in the difficulty of life and calling it theater.

When I looked at the pile of books building up in the living room in Trier—on the sofa where I read them when it rained, on the dining table where I puzzled over them and sometimes wrote back to them, in the deep windowsill where they ended up after lying on the garden table outside—I thought they are more than books. These volumes are objects. They are symbols, icons, like the saints overlooking me in every room in the house. Antonin Artaud, George Sand, Anaïs Nin, Sören Kierkegaard, Gustave Flaubert, Marcel Proust— above all Marcel Proust. They were not just writers. Their job was to be representations of themselves: so the rest of us can be reassured it is possible to be something other than framed within the bourgeoisie. Their job is to separate themselves from people at large. From society, so we may be attracted to the idea that individual thought is possible. *We are attracted by any life,* Proust wrote, *which represents for us something unknown and strange, by a last illusion still unshattered* (II:589). It is not that we love an illusion: it is that illusion is all we know. Reality is much harder to get hold of. If a writer suddenly breaks the spell, we may feel betrayed.

The lure of bohemia. Coffee stains. Abandoned ashes. Illicit sex in small wooden rooms. The sound of an accordion outside. If you turn into a bureaucrat, the magic is gone. I will not read you.

It was in those long afternoons, that grew

longer it seemed as summer progressed, when I had
these thoughts. In the small rose garden, which I
understood to be my private courtyard. I could not
walk in meditative circles like the former monks of
Bilbert monastery, but I was able to meander from
rose to rose, like a bumblebee or a hornet, whenever I
wished to stop reading. The thick volumes of Proust's
Remembrance weighted down the flimsy garden table by
my chair, which was getting rusty from being left out
in the rain. Sometimes you may read several pages of
Proust and at the end of it be surprised you were not
there yourself. It is a talent for recreation.

I took the liberty of fingering the petals of
the large rose blossoms. The white ones began to singe
into brown with time. The cherry-colored ones
retained their dangerous hue and freshness longer. I
stood there and looked over at the little table, the
book left open and upside down on top of another
volume. I recognized that everything went on aslant
this summer. I was in Germany to consider the writing of Mavis Gallant, specifically. Yet I had taken the
time to involve myself in Proust. My book on Gallant
would turn into a book on Proust. Yet it would not be
a book on Proust at all. *Remembrance of Things Past* is
only an opportunity. A site. A gathering place.

When Martin Heidegger wanted to discuss "Language in the Poem," he used the poetic work of George Trakl as an opportunity. It was not Trakl he wished to discuss: it was language and poetry. Something too general to float on its own. The specific work under discussion becomes the barge on which more general notions float. *We use the word "discuss" here to mean, first, to point out the place or site of something, to situate it, and second, to heed that place or site* (159). To Heidegger, the literary work is a compass. A campsite in a moist jungle. The kind of jungle where you may go for a walk, get lost, and die. Perhaps you die of a pre-existing condition, or else a new case of hypothermia, or even the emergence of a brown bear, fresh from hibernation. Such conditions as one might find in Canada.

Our discussion speaks of George Trakl only in that it thinks about the site of his poetic work, Heidegger writes (159). I not only want to remember this notation. I want to repeat it: so I do not end up feeling as negligent as I do feel. Marcel Proust's work is my site. For now. Heidegger writes that *Originally the word "site" suggests a place in which everything comes together, is concentrated. The site gathers unto itself, supremely and in the extreme. Its gathering power penetrates and pervades everything. The site, the gathering power, gathers in and preserves all it has gathered, not like an encapsulating shell but rather by penetrating with its light all it has gathered, and only thus releasing it into its own nature* (159–60).

I am glad it can be that way. I recognize that the garden itself, with its roses and rose leaves, its encompassing walls no one can climb over, its out-of-control grass, its clumsy brick patio, is the actual site. The garden that takes all things into itself and keeps them. Preserves occurrences in its embrace and emits them again in the fragrance of the rose.

Even though I could see over the vineyard from the gables in the upstairs bedroom, my townhouse lay in a middle-class neighborhood. In spite of the tomb-like ambiance suggested by the thick walls and unforgiving wooden shutters and a front door so large, thick, and heavy it could not be opened easily, the house reminded most of the structured middle-class life of the *Bürger*. The sheltered life of the *Bürgerin*. Above all, the house suggested containment and shelter. Even the garden, with its high rock walls, was a place of protection and shelter. The saints in their robes. The crosses with the tortured man on them. The predictability of the mail wagon and the schoolchildren.

I could not explain the discomfort I felt. It would sound foolish if I told of it, but I began to fear the house and the life I was meant to lead there. An extreme discomfort I could not pin down. There was a shower in the stone-walled bathroom which was loud and harsh, and no shower curtain. I would stand under the furious waterfall, soaking my hair, face, shoulders, all of me hoping the sheer force of the shower would wash away my apprehension. But it did not. I had begun to recognize the separation between me and continental Europe: that in my Danish mind there were only light birch trees and ash forests and galloping deer and straw-thatched roofs. Nothing prepared me for the stone walls of this Roman tradition that encloses its prison house around you. The world of the gothic, this one I was in, was something I did not understand. I found myself standing in the shower one evening, surprised to discover I had burst into tears. And once begun, I could not stop crying.

Having recognized the nature of my emotion, fear, and found a name for the stage setting of my personal theatre, gothic, I wanted to understand what it was. Fredric Jameson, in *The Cultural Logic of*

Late Capitalism, calls the gothic a *boring and exhausted paradigm* (289). But his explanation of what it is is not so boring: *on an individualized level—a sheltered woman of some kind is terrorized and victimized by an "evil" male* (289). He focuses on the idea of the shelter, shelteredness, as the central feature of the gothic: *Gothics are indeed ultimately a class fantasy (or nightmare) in which the dialectic of privilege and shelter is exercised: your privileges seal you off from other people, but by the same token they constitute a protective wall through which you cannot see, and behind which therefore all kinds of envious forces may be imagined in the process of assembling, plotting, preparing to give assault; it is, if you like, the shower-curtain syndrome (alluding to Hitchcock's* Psycho) (289).

The lure of bohemia turns out to be more than an attraction. The purpose of the artist is to lead the observer out of her prison house. It is the prison house imposed on women: the one that makes a woman reject the advances of a lover. Because the lover represents middle-class marriage. Jameson explains that the gothic's *classical form turns on the privileged content of the situation of middle-class women—the isolation, but also the domestic idleness, imposed on them by newer forms of middle-class marriage* (289).

I cannot help remembering Anaïs Nin's description of the pictures of Janko Varda: *In his landscape of joy women became staminated flowers, and flowers women. They were as fragrant as if he had painted them with thyme, saffron, and curry. They were translucent and airy, carrying their Arabian Nights cities like nebulous scarves around their Lucite necks* (4:242).

It remains no less obvious, writes Jean Cocteau in "The Justification for Injustice," *that there are those capable of giving offence, and those who must swallow it* (111). I was aware that I would rather be the offensive one. My body knew something I did not: by bursting into tears, I had to acknowledge I was being spoken to. I dried off and picked up the telephone. It was so easy to dial my lover's number. When he answered I said "take me away from here."

But it was more than the intimation of the gothic which was foreign to me. More than the barrier of language, so even watching a movie on television became an intellectual effort, an exercise in translation and retranslation. More, even, than the frustrating aggressiveness of a lover who drives up to the door in the evenings with noise. It was my work. Even though Mavis Gallant had my mornings, and frequently evenings, she did not become clear to me. On the hard, Victorian sofa I read through her *Paris Notebooks* and recognized the large distance between Paris in the sixties and Trier in the nineties. The difference was not time. It was the urban environment in Gallant's writing. So I was drawn to Proust instead, whose narrative, while further removed, was closer. Perhaps it was simply a space of mind.

When I read all the commentary on Gallant in the library, and there was a fair amount of it, I noticed none of her commentators and critics had understood her either. An essence was not coming through. It is, perhaps, an essence of doubt. What makes a work of art go from being good to great: the presence of doubt. It is not something directly spoken in the narrative; it is a thing you feel when you are in the presence of the text. Like a vague scent of blossom somewhere. The sorrow of knowing at the last moment you have failed. For this reason, photographs frequently show writers as pensive and sad. They know something you do not: that the work you admire is really a failure. Because language itself fails. There may not be words for the ambition of what you wish to utter. Susan Howe, in *My Emily Dickinson*, calls language *mutilated*. In speaking of Robert Browning and Emily Dickinson, she explains how they felt about their own writing: *Driven by enormous intellectual ambition into the vicinity of the mutilated message of all poetry, they fear the failure of their own energy* (84). Perhaps it is that sense of "mutilation" I cannot see in Gallant.

That after all, one is in the vicinity of sorrow. Someone like Dostoevsky, about whom Julia Kristeva writes in *Black Sun: Biographers point out that Dostoevsky preferred the company of those who were prone to sorrow. He cultivated it in himself and exalted it in both his texts and his correspondence* (176). That if you have spent a long time with such people, with their writing, you pick it up like a disease. The diseased reader.

It is about the Trier graffitist. A woman in her eighties who writes sentences on walls, murals, bridges, fences. Not sorrowful, but angry. I recognize what I am doing is inside a European tradition: I read within the classical arena. There are precedents, forerunners, a line of thought that can be traced. I am tracing that line, as I would the string in a cobweb a spider created between the leg of the garden chair and the table. I am finding my feet inside the tradition: the foot of a woman reading the classical score.

That the graffitist belongs to something called "outsider art." Even though there is no such thing as "outsider," she is among the artists and writers who belong to no tradition at all. Or perhaps they do, but their tradition is not codified. Naïf writing. Naïf because there is no consciousness in it of artistic value. In an essay called "Toward an Outsider Aesthetic," Roger Cardinal writes that the Outsider is *one who often has no conception of his or her work as art* (33). He believes that *creativity alters its character once the creator is made aware of the expectations or aesthetic standards of other people* (33). For this reason, her writing was necessarily of interest. I noticed that graffiti writing is not transmitted as a disease, but rather enforces a certain power in the reader.

❧

On occasion, Marcel Proust disguises the word *love*. He says "love" but means a kind of addiction. When the boy Marcel is in love with Gilberte, he is addicted to the chance of seeing her once a day in the Champs-Elysées. He watches the weather intensely to see if it is a day Gilberte will be out. He writes: *I no longer thought of anything save not to let a single day pass without seeing Gilberte* (1:433). This syndrome, this addiction that persists with people throughout life, is something the reader instinctively recognizes. That mental framework is also a site, a region of hysteria and terror that parades under the banner of love. The site of domestic abuse. The one thing contemplatives avoid: addiction to an individual other. It is a sensibility capable of cruelty. Even when so young, Proust recognizes the discord. He says his addiction to his meetings with Gilberte was so strong *that once, when my grandmother had not come home by dinnertime, I could not resist the instinctive reflection that if she had been run over in the street and killed, I should not for some time be allowed to play in the Champs-Elysées* (1:433).

I wonder how often one can be reminded of this and still not know it. *When one is in love, one has no love left for anyone,* he says (1:433). It is about the cruelty of lovers. The monomaniacal lover stalking his prey.

I was not in love, so I was free. In the train station, I changed money. I bought a copy of *Der Spiegel.* I had a cup of strong coffee. Travelers went from one place to another in the station, and I noticed they were not in a hurry. The platforms where we stood waiting for the arrival of the train were a passive place. People stood there in an oddly content-ed way. When the train arrived, I boarded and seated myself in an empty carriage next to the window. The only other passenger was seated on the other side, next to the window. The train moved out of town and into the rolling countryside toward Luxembourg. We struck up a conversation because we were alone in the car-riage. The other passenger was a gentleman from Israel, in Germany for the first time.

It occurred to me to wonder how we misrep-resent ourselves to each other. Often this is done without our knowledge. We assume to know what we

do not know. I could tell, for example, that my col-
leagues in Trier thought the graffitist was comical.
They were not laughing, but simply dismissive. I
could not help thinking of a story Jean Cocteau tells
in his diary about a priest in a hotel *who takes a dying
man's groans for erotic ones, and raps on the wall instead of coming to his aid* (91).

Yet I find it odd that Cocteau should use
that story to illustrate our distance from one another.
We commonly say we need to understand one another. Misunderstanding is negative. But such an idea
assumes we are capable of empathy. Perhaps we are
not. Perhaps each of us lives in a world no one else
can be privy to. How else can one explain history?
The history of the world: the book that K's accuser
has to write. If Job wishes to know the case against
him, perhaps it is here. It was all a misunderstanding.
The suggestion is that God misunderstood our inten-
tions.

It has often been pointed out that misrepre-
sentation is erotic. Our ability to participate erotically
depends on our capacity for play. For drama: theater.

That we wish to be someone else at that moment or to be seen as someone else. It is the conversation with the *other*. We not only need an other, we wish to be that other. At least, one would think so from reading. In *The Seducer's Diary*, Sören Kierkegaard's narrator, Johannes, corresponds with Cordelia, his fiancée. He thinks she is getting bored with the engagement. He agrees and concedes that a formal engagement is really a partition between them. *Only in opposition is there freedom,* he writes. *Only when no outsider suspects it does the love acquire meaning. Only when every stranger believes the lovers hate each other is love happy* (358).

That the resting point for erotic love is in opposition. So lovers argue.

One would think lovers were poets. That poets hold up the play of oppositions that exists in lovers' relationships and bring it into language itself. I had a vague sense that what was missing in the life of the *Bürgerin* I had taken on in Trier was the resolute boredom of life along rigid lines. The boredom of daily existence, which glared at me every morning. The predictability of small-town life: you know what day the gardener will cut your grass. You know at what hour the neighbor's door opens and closes. You hear the sound before it occurs.

That this lifestyle subsists on the exclusion of poetic language. The marginalization of Bohemia, of "outsider art" remaining "outsider." In her essay "The Ethics of Linguistics" in *Desire in Language,* Julia Kristeva talks about this juncture between society and language, society and its books. She critiques Roman Jakobson's reading of poets in 1930s Russia: his essay "The Generation That Wasted Its Poets." The article was read as *an indictment of a society founded on the murder of its poets* (31). But she expands on Jakobson: one may say this about all societies rigidly bourgeois. *Consequently,* Kristeva writes, *we have this Platonistic acknowledgment on the eve of Stalinism and fascism: a (any) society may be stabilized only if it excludes poetic language* (31).

She also acknowledges that *poetic language alone carries on the struggle against such a death, and so harries, exorcises, and invokes it* (31). Poetic language flirts with its nemesis: social order. *The question is unavoidable,* she asserts: *if we are not on the side of those whom society wastes in order to reproduce itself, where are we?* (31)

It occurs to me the "wasted poets" are the outsiders that cannot be let in: not because they are mad, like Artaud and van Gogh. The myth of the mad artist. But because they see more clearly. The social order is not clarity of vision; it is just social order. If you let an artist in, the clarity of seeing that occurs can only break the spell of the middle class and leave the helpless Bürgers stranded in the blinding light. *This is the torrid truth of the sun at two o'clock in the afternoon* (499), Artaud says of van Gogh. *There are no ghosts in the paintings of van Gogh, no visions, no hallucinations* (499). It is a world so clear you cannot be held captive in myth and paranoia: there is nothing gothic, no terror except in what is unblinkingly clear. You are free to enter the nightmare of reality. *A slow generative nightmare gradually becoming clear* (499). Seeing this way, you are in no one's power but your own. So the vision of clarity needs to be wasted or society cannot be controlled.

The discomfort I felt in my townhouse, —in the library, in the streets of the village, everywhere except the rose garden itself—must, I thought, be part of this picture. I did not find myself weeping in the shower for no reason. Instead, I had intimations of that "slow generative nightmare" that tells you the way society is organized has nothing to do with reality. And reality is largely unknown.

I did not think about this any further. The morning after I called my lover on the telephone, he picked me up and drove me to Frankfurt. Before I knew it, I was home: in another country, in my own house, buried in my own work in the office. It took another three years to turn the pages of that book back to where I was.

It was at a picnic with a friend of a friend of mine. We went to a park by the oceanside. There was a table close to the water. It was evening and golden sunshine gleamed on the lightly rippling surface, where a few children were jumping and swimming. Their calls and shouts could be heard, coming from what seemed like a great distance. There were not many people in the park. It was the end of a hot day. All was still; not a single gust of wind stirred in the tall fir trees towering over us. I spread a red-checkered table cloth over the table, napkins, plates, and wine glasses. My friend's friend took out a bottle of white wine. She poured the glasses full and I looked at the bottle. It was Mosel wine. From Bernkastel.

In a flash, the entire summer, in all its details, its smells and sounds and texture—welled back into my mind. It was of course at Bernkastel that I walked, intrigued, into the courtyard of the old monastery, thinking of enclosures for classical thought. What both Cocteau and Heidegger might describe as a slippery slope of errors you cannot escape, once you are on it. I have misnamed the town on purpose: in an attempt to turn real experience into fiction. I have named the mythical village Bilbert. But it was not mythical at all. It was Bernkastel, situated on the slopes of the Mosel River, flanked by the sticks and stilts and trellises of vineyards. So real, in fact, that I could sit at a picnic table half a world away, a red-checkered table cloth and a plate of salad and glass of white wine, and at the first taste be instantly transported back.

At that moment I was watching the sunset behind the hills on the other side of the inlet. We were now two women in a park, after being one

woman in a garden. The evening grew more peaceful.
The families seated in small groups round about
packed up and moved on. Soon we were the last pic-
nickers except for a small group that had set their
lawn chairs on the sand and were dragging on the
evening languorously. I thought again, after having
thought it so many times before, how pleasant it is to
be lifted out of the squirming discomforts of social
life as we know it. Of culture as we know it: all cul-
tures. Codes that impose their rigidity on you and
keep you from being free. The enforcers of these
codes: the company of men. How much more gentle,
airy, light, free, and empowering is the company of
women. No arguments, no manipulations, no veiled
criticisms and damaging innuendoes. Just a good time:
a joke, a laugh, a good story.

All of history, the book that K's accuser
needs to write, attests to the truth of Heidegger's
slope of errors. Errors build on one another. The classical tradition feeds on itself and produces more classical works. Classical because presumably valid for all
times. It is called culture and becomes something
worth waging war over. That culture is conditioned by
notions of theology: that tell us we are guilty at birth.
We look around and do not know what it was we did.

What our punishment is. Everything appears to be a strange circus. What would happen if the woman, the audience for all this, left? As Hélène Cixous and Catherine Clément say in "The Guilty One," if she just *Quits the show? Ends the circus in which too many women are crushed to death* (56). They dream in their text *The Newly Born Woman: She has loosed herself from the looks fixed upon her . . . she has loosed herself from the ties that bound her to those showmen . . . all the masters* (57).

But I am not alone: the woman I speak of is not alone in wishing to "loose herself" from history. After being "crushed to death" for so long, how does she re-emerge? Find the garden that releases her? It is a symptom of the present to wish for this release.

Fredric Jameson thinks the word for this is "postmodernism," which he explains. In *The Cultural Logic of Late Capitalism,* he points out the empowering effect of this new scheme of thought. He writes, *I think we now have to talk about the relief of the postmodern generally, a thunderous unblocking of logjams and a release of new productivity that was somehow tensed up and frozen, locked like cramped muscles, at the latter end of the modern period* (313).

And what was the modern, then? In the eyes of the postmodern, the modern represents *a long period of ossification and dwelling among dead monuments* (313).

But when you look again, the monuments of the past are not so dead after all. We write the obituaries too soon. We bury them alive. We are jolted out of the newly contented present: the pleasant supper in a park, shaded by tall trees, free of innuendoes, by the sudden appearance of a bottle of wine. It is a bottle your friend's friend innocently brought. Wine so good only because it took a long time to perfect. Centuries, even. And the taste of the wine itself brings back memories you did not think about in your effort to be free.

It is a condition re-enacted in the life of every individual. It is something Marcel Proust is famous for having noticed. When he speaks of literature, he thinks he cannot see what is important, and therefore has no gift for literature. *Always I was incapable of seeing anything for which a desire had not already been roused in me by something I had read* (II:139), he writes. Had he not read it, he would not have noticed. Therefore he thinks he would make a poor writer. *How often,* he continues, *have I remained incapable of bestowing my attention upon things or people that later, once their image has been presented to me in solitude by an artist, I would have travelled many miles, risked death to find again!* (II:737) That it takes the presence of the artist, even when the artist is a vintner and his art is wine, to remind you: there was something there you left behind.

That what was highlighted throughout the summer in Germany and France was the continuous need for escape. When I was at home, encompassed by thick walls and the complete absence of erudition, I could escape into the rose garden and hear Proust's easily flowing sentences. As though he had been talking on those pages for countless decades, and like an eternally revolving wheel was unable to stop. No matter what the subject—trivial chatter at a social gathering, or morose thoughts in his solitary bedroom, or a silly conversation on the telephone—all was absorbed in his easy language and transmitted onto the endless page. Chimes that continued to ring, even here in my garden, so late in the century. Then I could also escape the town I lived in and go to another, where I was still a stranger and could wander in happy anonymity. Or I could escape to another country: to Luxembourg or France, and pretend it was all a vacation. There was nothing serious. Nothing hinged on whether I came or went.

The tug-of-war between enclosure and escape became objectively interesting to me. This phenomenon actually kept me awake at night. It was a curious feature of that whole summer that I did not sleep. I followed the routine of all other people in town and shut my lights off at eleven or sometimes twelve at night. The shutters were down and the streets were quiet. The bedroom was upstairs, and like many European houses, the room followed the pattern of the roof. The ceilings leaned inward toward their apex at the center, which meant one could stand straight only in the center of the room. The bed was tucked in under the leaning walls, so it was necessary to crouch low in order to crawl into bed. I lay in the wooden box that passed for a bed, with an uneven, lumpy straw mattress, looking at the window set in the gable. Eventually, I got up again. I put on my robe and went downstairs. All was very quiet. It became a habit to cut myself a piece of thick nutty rye bread, butter it, and have a midnight snack at the small kitchen table. I thought of a comment made by Stanley Fish at the end of his chapter on "Critical Self-Consciousness" in *Doing What Comes Naturally*. He reflects that *It is because history is inescapable that every historical moment—that is, every moment—feels so much like an escape* (467).

That I was fooling myself thinking I was doing the escaping. To feel like you got away: that was simply an inescapable feeling brought on by an inescapable fact: that one lives in history. Fish goes on at length about another inescapable condition: that *change cannot be engineered, neither can it be stopped* (463).

It is at night, when one is further enclosed by darkness and entrapment seems complete, that the mind plays freely. What plays is everything one has heard and read. There is apparently no limit to how much the mind takes in. There is a limit to how much of it becomes conscious, at any given moment, but beneath what we can recognize is there, a thousand other thoughts are lurking. It is a condition the so-called postmodernists have not only noticed, but made much of, that we are not so original in our thoughts.

In that mental cage, which is not a cage but a freely open universe, there are all the texts we have come across and imprinted there. The mind is a perfect scanner, scanning page after page. What we see and hear is permanently imprinted there. *And I have never encountered a logic that seemed to me anything but borrowed* (144), says Artaud in his essay "In Total Darkness" as early as 1927.

There were two rooms in the small upstairs floor of my townhouse. One was the bedroom, where it was necessary to crawl into bed. The other was a study. Unlike the bedroom, the study had high ceilings except for the extreme edges, where the room sloped inward. It was truly a garret, the kind depicted in drawings of nineteenth-century poets dying of tuberculosis, etching out their last heartfelt laments. There was a desk in one corner, facing the window in the attic gable. The window was in the ceiling above the desk, leaning with the wall, so on looking out one could detect the red roof of the house opposite, higher on the hill.

Sometimes I went into the study and wondered what I should use it for. As it was, the whole house had become my study and I did not need a separate room. But it had the feel of a private place, so it became a correspondence room. When I walked in there, it felt like I should have a private conversation with an intimate. I wrote letters to my friends at the desk. The act of writing these letters became important, as though serious events hinged on the missives I produced. I had to articulate my daily life. It was becoming noticeable to me that, for all practical purposes, I was not there. No one knew I was there. If I did not say so, put my life into words, it would somehow not exist. I would not exist. I was afraid of my nonexistence without exactly knowing that was how I felt. That writing it would make it happen was not a new idea. The need to articulate has been speculated on richly in European thought. I knew that. I respected that, and so, I did not mock myself. *Language is the house of Being,* wrote Heidegger (63). *Something is only where the appropriate and therefore competent word names a thing as being . . .* (63). Or, *The being of anything that is resides in the word* (63).

When it rained, the window over my head filled with raindrops. I could hear them splattering on the pane in my small garret.

In *Either/Or,* Sören Kierkegaard has a peculiar passage about the art of forgetting and the art of remembering. I returned to that page several times in order to reflect on how I thought about my life in Germany. Everything there was so vividly remembered, yet I could not say I remembered anything in particular. It was a situation, a place, and a time I both wanted to remember and forget. It was the idea I wanted to remember, perhaps. Life in Germany should have been better than it was. Romance in France should have been more intense than it was. I suspected myself of fictionalizing for the sake of my own memory.

The small, unexpected moments are what I remember with pleasure. I remember sitting in a courtyard café in the evening with my lover. We were putting an end to a hot day. Our table was in the shade of a leafy tree, and the white Mosel wine in our big glasses was cold. We were waiting for the closest thing to a salad the German chef could make. I remember the moment because my friend was too tired to be intense and romantic. For once, he was calm, slightly absent, not on my case. He was just a friend at that moment, something I suspected he should have been all along. Just a friend. It seemed I had to go through so much fury in order to get to such soothing spaces with him.

I remember setting eyes on the secret garden of the monks at Bernkastel. It was just a fleeting moment, full of shade on a warm day. Those seconds are like floodgates. You open them and a thousand other waters rush in. I thought of all secret gardens. Places where you go deeply into thought, not just your own, but the thought of your whole community. Here it was the Christian Fathers. I remembered my rose garden. Not just the blooming roses and their vague perfume. But the books. I remember the stack of books and how I dipped into them like a pool in the afternoon shade.

Kierkegaard writes that *The more poetically one remembers, the more easily one forgets, for remembering poetically is really just an expression of forgetfulness. In remembering poetically, what was experienced has already undergone a change in which it has lost all that was painful* (234). Perhaps I have singled out those moments for their poetic value and have changed them to soothe an otherwise discordant summer. That I find small pools of tranquillity because everything else was confusing and a bit painful. But to Kierkegaard, there is a lesson in that observation. He says that *To remember in this way, one must be careful how one lives, especially how one enjoys* (234). I do not know if I was careful. I do not know if it is possible to be careful in that way.

This leads me to the thought of what was, in fact, painful. Because I am not unaware that I could be telling all this differently. I could be telling a story, the story of my summer in Germany. It would have a beginning, a middle, and an end. A good story, perhaps. I would be the protagonist, but not the heroine. I would come out rather vanquished. Because something happens to a telling when it becomes a story. Suddenly, there must be opposition. Hélène Cixous and Catherine Clément state emphatically that *Thought has always worked through opposition* (63). Like He/She or Father/Mother or High/Low. *Through dual, hierarchical oppositions. Superior/Inferior* (64). *Everywhere (where) ordering intervenes* (64).

A woman alone can come out a "victor" in a story only when the reader concedes to poetic language. Otherwise, what happens in a plotted narrative works to the advantage of the male character. This is so because, as Cixous and Clément say, *We see that "victory" always comes down to the same thing: things get hierarchical. Organization by hierarchy makes all conceptual organizations subject to man* (64). I mention this only because I found myself at a disadvantage. I was a woman alone. I was a guest in another country. I was at the mercy of my hosts.

In a few short words, I have discovered a set of experiences that always occur to women in the position I have said I was in. These experiences include: she is set up; she is presumed upon; she is foisted upon others; she is approached as if she were a battleground, assaulted either for love or for victory. Meanwhile, she says nothing. She does nothing to undermine her assailant. Instead, she quietly goes home and lets stories go whichever way they please. Because she knows she cannot control the stories men tell each other. Nor does she wish to.

She does not exist, write Cixous and Clément, *she can not-be; but there has to be something of her. He keeps, then, of the woman on whom he is no longer dependent, only this space, always virginal, as matter to be subjected to the desire he wishes to impart* (65). In retrospect, I think those are fine words.

But I also know, in retrospect, the world will never think so. It will never occur to anyone, seriously, that our very logocentrism ousts the woman from the central story. She must be there as the opposition, or as the margin that frames the picture.

For this reason, my friends are the poets. I am loyal to the poets because they see outside the story. They vie for credibility in a world where poetry is not credible. Readers may presume on the poet, may suspect his or her integrity. May freely slander the poet because of the language used. So Antonin Artaud wrote in a letter to George Soulié de Morant on February 17, 1932, a Thursday morning, that *nothing is so odious and painful, nothing so agonizing for me as doubt cast on the reality and nature of the phenomena I describe* (287). There is good reason to fear what has come to be known among women as "crazy-making." Above all, she must be sane, reasonable, cool, and comforting.

Speaking of Emily Dickinson, Susan Howe suggests that *In the Theatre of the Human Heart, necessity of*

poetic vocation can turn creator to corruptor (108). "Poetic vocation" is not simply the act of writing poetry. It is also the act of reading. Of finding poetic language in the midst of "mechanical empiricism." The vocation of responding to another language when it appears. There is a suggestion that the woman reading is the woman corrupting. Wherever she goes, intentionally or not, she disturbs, corrupts, the comfortable logos that was there before.

All she did was sit and study. Why was there so much commotion in her wake? *Dickinson was expert in standing in corners,* Susan Howe says, *expert in secret listening and silent understanding* (116).

After being deeply embroiled in social life for three oversized volumes, Marcel Proust, the narrator of *Remembrance of Things Past,* decides to withdraw from society in order to attend to his writing. It is an uncharacteristic move and one which his friends and acquaintances are unlikely to sympathize with. He has to make strong resolutions. He tells himself, *Certainly it was my intention to resume next day, but this time with a purpose, a solitary life. So far from going into society, I would not*

even permit people to come and see me at home during my hours of work, for the duty of writing my book took precedence now over that of being polite or even kind (III: 1035). Like the lover, the writer has no time for anyone. He has gone from lover to writer, and the configurations are the same. His book has been with him all this time, like an intimation, but he did not recognize it. The way you are with a person with whom you are not yet in love. And why should friends and acquaintances sympathize with the writer? It is not a particularly sympathetic undertaking. Also one that is hard to explain. Marcel resolves to explain as accurately as possible. He says, *But I should have the courage to reply to those who came to see me or tried to get me to visit them that I had, for necessary business which required my immediate attention, an urgent, a supremely important appointment with myself* (III:1035).

He concludes this will look like egotism to other people. But he does not say what the more far-reaching conclusion will be. It is only an appointment with himself while he is writing. Later, it is an appointment with the reader. On the other side, the reader will behave like the writer. She will not have time for anyone else. Suddenly, she will have a pressing appointment with a book, while her lover argues about loyalties. The argument will fall on deaf ears.

The reader will then be infected with the disease of the book being read. As with all infectious illnesses, she will be caught in its bonds unconsciously. She does not know she has a disease. But she goes on to write a consequent text, borne of the text she has read. But it will not be another auto-representational novel. It will be what Linda Hutcheon, in "The Metafictional Paradox," calls *anti-representation* (137). It will be a text that remains outside the novel genre. And outside the critical genre. It will be unidentifiable: because it was a disease to begin with. A new virus, something like AIDS.

Speaking of the *nouveau nouveau roman*, that French invention Proust has been accused of generating, Hutcheon writes that there are *very serious implications of this particular mode of metafiction for the novel genre itself. And it would appear that it is not so much a matter of intense textual self-consciousness being self-destructive, or leading to the death of the novel; it is rather a case of its suggesting a further but different stage—anti-representation—which, usually for ideological reasons, would deny mimesis and even diegesis* (136–137). The writer of such metafiction, who was the reader of fiction, does not want her text to resemble anything from real life. What must the reader of the reader's text then do? Hutcheon says that *When this stage is reached, one requires the extra-textual aid of the author* (137).

The town of Trier was frequently crowded. Especially in the downtown area, where the tourists congregated and marched and sauntered. The locals joined the tourists on their rounds, probably out of curiosity. Every sidewalk, courtyard, and plaza was given over to sidewalk and terrace cafés. The chairs and tables were always full, coffees and beers on all the tables. To walk through the downtown streets was a matter of wading past thousands of eaters and drinkers. The university area, where I went every day, was also crowded. But there it was full of cotton-clad students in wool sweaters and large, sensible, leather walking shoes. The busses were always full. The town parks were filled with people relaxing. There were no vacant parking spaces.

There were times when I allowed myself to get lost in the crowds. Perhaps downtown, among books at the book stalls or striking up a conversation with someone at a terrace café. But the scene never seemed quite real. It was not real life going on there, the daily necessities and routines acted out by the populace. Instead, it was Americans with cameras or Italians with loud voices marauding about as if the town were a playground. And the old buildings had been renovated to appear more worthy as time pieces. One Canadian writer, a friend who happened to be there one week, expressed the opinion that downtown Trier looked like a Disney scam. I often found it strange, like wearing clothes that do not quite fit, that I would not be going "home" with my friends when they appeared. "Home" for me was up that hill, just above the valley, just as you leave the downtown area in the direction of the university.

I preferred to be away from the confusing crowds. In retrospect, I do not think I was "anti-social" so much as I was getting slightly perverse. Moribund. Saying "no" to most things, just when there was this plenty around. I would find myself in my small garden, staring transfixed at a rose. It would be off-white, fading at the edges, singed by age to a dirty brown.

Perhaps, as Proust says, I had a kind of

appointment with myself. But it was a meeting of a different nature. I was not engaged in the act of writing a book. There was just a question I needed to ask myself. The question was so unfocused, I did not exactly know what it was. I wondered, for example, about the woman who wishes to be alone. Is it different from when the man wishes to be so? The idea of solitude has been dignified for men by the great thinkers. But I could not escape the suspicion that the women who choose solitude in our literature come out of it a little odd. Perhaps I was imagining things. I found solace of a kind in what people like Kierkegaard—whose solitude does in fact appear odd, whose whole narrative titled *Either/Or* is surprisingly cruel and manipulative, even when it is brilliant—have written. Kierkegaard's narrator asserts in a letter to a friend, that *When around me all has become still, solemn as a starlit night, when the soul is all alone in the world, there appears before it not a distinguished person, but the eternal power itself. It is as though the heavens parted, and the I chooses itself—or, more correctly, it accepts itself* (491).

To accept oneself: perhaps that is a taller order than it seems. Paradoxically, the reader may encounter herself in so many books which, on the surface, appear to have nothing in common with her.

What I am writing here is an account of something that may strike the observer as non-narrative. Because there is no discernible progress from one event to another. This observer was expecting story, perhaps. But already by the advent of the *nouveau roman,* we could see the possibility of the internal story. A character may be doing nothing, outwardly: she may be sitting in a rose garden reading. The only movement in the scene might be a bee flying among the flowers. Or a gentle breeze suddenly brushing the corner of the page. Everything that happens does so in the mind of the reader. That, in itself, might constitute a story. In his chapter on rhetoric, for example, Stanley Fish wishes to say *that something is always happening to the way we think* (501). It is perhaps impossible to exist without something taking place. To be outside of story would be to not exist.

What confuses is that stories never end. Fictions are false because they provide false endings. There is always a next day: just as the idea of the end of the universe can never gain currency, since it is forever trailed by the question of what is behind the end of the universe. In fiction, we strive for a last word of some kind. The same happens in theory and philosophy. It is, Stanley Fish wishes to say, *a tug-of-war between two views of human life and its possibilities, no one of which can ever gain complete and lasting ascendancy because in the very moment of its triumphant articulation each turns back in the direction of the other* (501).

In saying this much, he proceeds to discount reader-response criticism, feminism, Marxism, and Freudianism. *Here one might speak of the return of the repressed,* Fish writes. *Were it not that the repressed—whether it be the fact of difference or the desire for its elimination—is always so close to the surface that it hardly need be unearthed* (501). It would seem he wishes to eliminate all dialogue and give the last word to himself. He writes: *What we seem to have is a tale full of sound and fury, and signifying itself, signifying a durability rooted in inconclusiveness, in the impossibility of there being a last word* (501). It occurs to me Fish might think of the Trier graffitist as a bag of hot air. So, too, is Marcel Proust. From opposite sides of our dialogism comes a "tale full of sound and fury." But empty at the core. This view strikes me as profoundly unsympathetic to human experience. Fish's remarks have the flavor of the atom bomb: since no one can win, we simply eliminate them all.

In this context, I am reminded of Antonin Artaud's comments about a new "tragedy" he had just written. In a letter to André Gide on February 10, 1935, he invites Gide to a reading of the text of his play. He explains that *The dialogue of this tragedy is, if I may say so, of the most extreme violence. And there is nothing among the traditional notions of Society, order, Justice, Religion, family and Country, that is not attacked* (340).

Then he adds, when considering audience response: *There must be no incidents* (340).

On the eve of the "shower-curtain syndrome," when I phoned my lover in Bonn and asked him to take me away from Germany, I was awake all night. There were brilliant stars in the sky, for it was a clear night. The silhouette of tall-gabled houses and the spires of churches stood out against the moonlight. When I went into the rose garden in the dark, the brilliance of bright green leaves shot through with sunlight, and starkly colored flowers that cheered up the afternoon so vividly, had dampened. The small garden now looked like a small garden enclosed by high stone walls. It was no longer a place of repose, but a kind of enclosure. I began to think of the rose in its prison, how in one day my perception had changed.

My sense of oppositions had come to haunt me as being purely symbolic. That there was an argument at all was now, in the unexpectedly final night in my house, doubtful. The books I had been reading, which I presumed to presume a male reader, and which I therefore did not read but "dipped into" the way a bee dips into a flower, did not presume such things at all. I thought of a remark made by Northrop Frye concerning the Bible. In *The Great Code* he suggests that *Wherever we have love we have the possibility of sexual symbolism. The kerygma, or proclaiming rhetoric, of the Bible is a welcoming and approaching rhetoric, addressed by a symbolically male God to a symbolically female body of readers* (231).

Next morning my friend arrived. My suitcase was packed and I was ready to go even before I opened the door. During the night, I had discharged all my social duties. I paid the rent for the rest of the summer, paid the telephone bill, handed the key over to my neighbor. In case I decided not to return. We drove from Trier to Frankfurt, and for once I was glad of the lightning speed at which my friend drove on the Autobahn. I listened to him talk all the way, like the humming of the engine of the car. Perhaps he was disappointed. If he was, he put a good face on it. He said I did not have him on a silver platter now like I did before. He would play harder to get. In fact, he would ask for a transfer to the other side of the Iron Curtain, which was no longer an Iron Curtain, where no one, and certainly not I, would ever go.

Paradoxically, in this light we were friendlier than before. My plane did not leave till the following morning, so he took me to a restaurant in Frankfurt. He ordered meals we would have to cook ourselves on cooking stones brought to the table. But he did the cooking. He stood up, rolled up his sleeves, and began flipping prawns, scallops, bits of cod into the air with more dexterity than a Japanese sushi chef. He put on a show and made me laugh. There were no arguments anymore, just a good time. The irony was not lost on me—that I had to actually leave for him to wake up to a relationship I suddenly really liked.

❧

Perhaps it is, when you think back over a period of time, whether three months or three years, that retrospective gives you a chance to fictionalize. That does not mean you alter the reality of what took place, if anything. Your ability to fictionalize the past has more to do with narrative time than with story. This is suggested nicely by Fredric Jameson in his chapter on "Video." In arguing why experimental video does not work with fictions, he defines fictions in terms of "fictive time" rather than story. *We all know,* he writes, *but always forget, that the fictive scenes and conversations on the movie screen radically foreshorten reality as the clock ticks and are never—owing to the now codified mysteries of the various techniques of film narrative—coterminous with the putative length of such moments in real life, or in "real time"* (74). We find videotapes that do not "foreshorten" "real time" irritating to watch. We go through the experience like the subject of daguerreotype. The photographer had a clamp to hold the subject's head in place for the ten minutes or so it took for the exposure.

Jameson writes: *Is it possible, then, that "fiction" is what is in question here and that it can be defined essentially as the construction of just such fictive and foreshortened temporalities (whether of film or reading), which are then substituted for a real time we are thereby enabled momentarily to forget?* (74) In that way, when you loop out of your "real life," into another existence, where things happen in reverse order, or happen too fast, or suddenly stand still like a bower of transcendence halting the universe in its course, you enter a world of fiction. Suddenly you are Alice in Wonderland. Or Dorothy in Oz. Everything is disproportionate and you become homesick for "real time."

But to Jameson, the consequence of his observation is theoretical. *The question of fiction and the fictive would thereby find itself radically dissociated from questions of narrative and storytelling as such,* he says (74). It seemed to me just then, on the eve of my departure, that we use fiction to escape the ennui of "real time," a condition so explored by the moderns. We also use the act of travel for the same purpose. Compared to fictive time, the time of our lives seems heavy and slow and monotonous.

It had occurred to me on a walk through the

vineyard below my townhouse in Trier that it might be true, what Virginia Woolf confessed to be the usefulness of women. Women are mirrors, she says. *Whatever may be their use in civilised societies, mirrors are essential to all violent and heroic action. That is why Napoleon and Mussolini both insist so emphatically upon the inferiority of women, for if they were not inferior, they would cease to enlarge* (36). As we walked there, on the winding path to the ruins of the old wine press, I realized I was my lover's mirror. That was why he talked so much and I listened so much. It must become infuriating for him when I cease to listen.

But more, I suspected myself of acting as the mirror for the texts I read. In the stillness of the garden, under a blanket of sun, the narratives of Proust and Kierkegaard and Artaud and also Nin and Kristeva, found a reflection in me which, like a mirror left under the glare of the sunbeam, must eventually ignite. In the meantime, the language of them all became enlarged.

For this reason, also, Frye's Bible might be assumed to exist before a body of female readership. It is a big surprise for the classical culture, which has absorbed its own protestations, when the mirror cracks and splits the text in two. Much of the material of the texts has leaked into the crack and been absorbed by the body that reposes there.

But all readers act as mirrors to words. It is an inevitable outcome. Words are not people. Heidegger suggests that words are more than words. In *On the Way to Language,* Heidegger says the gods appear to human beings through words, the way the gods appear to you in Nordic mythology only through an oak tree. *The approach of the god took place in Saying itself* (139), he writes. Further, *Saying was in itself the allowing to appear of that which the saying ones saw because it had already looked at them* (139). You can utter words because a god has looked at you. The word, the poetic word, is the gods looking at you, having looked at you.

However this may be meant, there is a transcendent element to language which appears to exist outside both form and content. It may be in voice itself. But when a thought is well articulated, there is a spark that does not escape the reader. That is why the texts are so mesmerizing. Certain texts become more important than the reader's immediate surroundings.

Daily life goes into the shadows for a while, and the sun shines on some other reality the reader has begun to glimpse. That other reality has little if anything to do with the subject matter of the text.

On the poet's side, *Is anything more exciting and more dangerous for the poet than his relation to words?* asks Heidegger (141). Is writing not analogous to working with fissionable material? Something radioactive, for which you need gloves?

For this reason lovers give each other words. It is the best gift a lover can receive. The most generous gift. So they write each other letters. The recipient keeps the letters, envelopes and all, and ties them together in a red ribbon. Love letters become precious. They are hidden in special places, like talismans: something with magic powers.

Letters to friends are pale imitations of the love letter. But I clung to those imitations because I missed my friends. In the silence of the southern German evening, when the town had quieted down to television and chocolate deserts, I turned on the lamp

in the garret and phrased yet another letter. It is one
of the difficult things about being away from home
for a whole season: you make a life without your
friends and family. You try to go about your daily
business in the ensuing emptiness. The only loving
face you see is the face of the rose. Even if you have a
lover who is frequently at your side. He sits beside you
on the sofa in the overstuffed German living room.
He sits across from you at your kitchen table, eating
your vegetarian soup. He lies beside you on the wood-
en bed with the straw mattresses at night, and you are
aware of the sharply vaulted ceilings like a dagger over
your head. Even with a companion such as this, you
miss your friends.

So I felt sorry for the old age Proust
describes in "Within a Budding Grove," a time of life
when not even words can give pleasure. Proust's narrator says of himself: *I returned home. I had just spent the New
Year's Day of old men, who differ on that day from their juniors,
not because people have ceased to give them presents but because they
themselves have ceased to believe in the New Year* (1:526). Presents: words. Old people who have lost the pleasure of
receiving gifts. *Presents I had received,* he says, *but not that
present which alone could bring me pleasure, namely a line from
Gilberte* (1:526).

That to live outside of love is a form of "old age." But it is not actual old age, only symbolic. To be without the spark that gives its bearer joy is to live in anticipation of death. But to exist in the hopes of "a line" from a loved one, that is to anticipate life. Perhaps that summer in Germany, it was my sorrow to not be in love. In spite of that, I was in love. It was a condition not directed at a specific person, but something that found its central existence in the rose garden and which was transmitted in the words of innumerable writers.

The same rural people came every day into the town square of Trier and set up their stalls. There they sold vegetables grown on their farms: potatoes, beets, carrots, cabbage. Fresh eggs. Honey. The open-air stalls were integrated into the shopping sector of the town, and the faces behind them became familiar to those whose daily rounds went through the town center. These merchants existed outside the system of commerce otherwise sanctioned. They did not pay rent on their shops. They did not buy goods wholesale. They simply brought in what was on their property and took money in return. It occurred to me to view the farmer's market merchants as one would other artists operating outside the corporate system. Because in the arts, mainstream works are incorporated: absorbed, distributed, sold by corporations that profit by the exchange. So-called "outsider art" does not profit and there is often no exchange. Yet the "goods" are the same, and not infrequently "outsider" goods are the fresher.

I had come to view the Trier graffitist as a kind of "farmers market" of literature. When I rode on the bus, usually packed with those going shopping between the downtown and the suburbs, and with students going to and from school, and twice a day with workers going to and from work, I would end up reading her lines without exactly being aware I was reading them. "The Pope is a murderer of women!" "The Catholic church kills!" On occasion there were long paragraphs that took up a whole wall. "If you think you have escaped Fascism, you are wrong. Fascism is all around us. In your home, in your school, in your church. . . ." When I sat down on a bench in the town center, tired of walking for so long, I would find myself looking at one of her sentences, perhaps inscribed on the base of a beautiful water fountain, with angels pouring water out of celestial jars.

When I wished to know something more about what I was looking at, I picked up an essay titled "From Domination to Desire" by Eugene W. Metcalf, Jr. There I came on the following warning: *the designation of the art of certain people as "outsider" can be a result (and even, perhaps, a cause) of their social disempowerment. Touristically seeking authentic experience beyond the boundaries of social convention through confrontation with the antimodern Other, some supporters of Outsider Art, it can be argued, transform the mentally disturbed, impoverished, or simply isolated and unusual people into willful, antisocial heroes* (218). Even when sympathetic, the interested reader needs to guard against presuming on the object of her interest and thereby misrepresenting her. The only possibility left is to let the quotation, the graph, the song, stand on its own. Without commentary. Metcalf also states the consequence of unintended appropriation: *To the extent that they symbolically celebrate the very people they have, by implication, socially disempowered by defining them as deviant, many supporters of Outsider Art romanticize and trivialize the marginalization of these people* (218).

There was one thing that held an enchantment for me beyond others. That was the sound of

the bells of the great cathedral in central Strasbourg.
The cathedral is in itself extremely ornate and gothic,
and I did not relate to the filigree Catholicism of the
building. It was enough for me to say it was magnificent, but not particularly welcoming. The sound of
the bells was something else. When the Protestant
churches removed the decorations of Catholicism,
they left the bells alone. For this reason, I awoke to
the ringing of a thousand memories I had not heard
since childhood.

The place we stayed in while in Strasbourg
was close to the cathedral, and the sounds from the
cathedral square could be heard clearly. It was a small
apartment in a building at least three hundred years
old. The furniture was large for the small space. I
opened the tall window looking into the tops of trees
and birds vying for space there. Below, the foot traffic
of the narrow street bustled. The sun blared into the
room. The bells of the great cathedral rang. I could
not help remembering the village of my childhood.
On Sundays, the bells in all the steeples rang all
around town. First one began slowly, sonorously. Then
another in another church rang in a tenor clang. A
third joined in from the west end, piping an unde-
clared melody. A fourth church steeple, this one from

the Protestant cathedral on the hilltop, bonged over all the others. I listened to this as a child in the window, indefinite feelings welling up in my chest. I looked forward to the ringing of the village churches. Now, so many years later, this magnificent cathedral could not anticipate the thoughts of Protestantism its bells engendered.

I recalled something Proust had written about his recollection of the garden bell at Combray, at the end of his *Remembrance.* It was about how one could create a vantage point out of specific events for one's whole life. Speaking of his life and his memories of it all, he writes that *In this vast dimension which I had not known myself to possess, the date on which I had heard the noise of the garden bell at Combray—that far-distant noise which nevertheless was within me—was a point from which I might start to make measurements* (III:1106). An artificial point of origin. A theoretical True North in the compass of a "vast dimension" in which life takes place.

Even while writing his memoirs, Jean Cocteau declares he could never write his memoirs. *If the contents of our memory were able to materialize and roam*

about, he writes, *they would clutter up the entire world. How amazing, then, that such a clutter can fit into our brain* (149). Memory were better left as memory. As a kind of dream. As the fictions memories are. Like textual fiction, there are medieval memories, surreal memories, romantic memories, existential ones, dada ones. There are even postmodernist memories. They come in all genres.

Cocteau has categorized the memories of Marcel Proust as dream literature. His explanation is that *The instantaneous nature of dream is such that one can dream in the space of a second the equivalent of Marcel Proust's entire work. For that matter, Proust's work is closer to dream than what is commonly passed off as dream narrative. It has the innumerable cast, the shifting plots, the lack of chronological sequence, the cruelty, the dread, the comical, the precise set design, even the "all's-well-that-ends-badly"* (149).

Shifting plots, a large cast, lack of chronology, a surreal setting with every item accurately and weirdly in place, a bad ending. These must constitute a dream for Cocteau. It is a tragedy, this Proustian dream. Yet the reader does not realize it is a tragedy until too late.

It is possible that Cocteau's dream narrative is something more sinister. Proust's narrative is a tragedy because it is not a dream, but a hallucination. A waking dream. An episode under the influence of something else. There is a discussion of the relationship between (written) art and magic in Northrop Frye's *The Great Code.* Frye contends that there is a *long-standing connection between the written book and the arts of magic, and the way that the poetic impulse seems to begin in the renunciation of magic, or at least, of its practical aims* (227). The writer takes over from the magician. Perhaps because of the nature of the word—the power of language, as Heidegger might say. The written word, says Frye, *re-creates the past in the present, and gives us, not the familiar remembered thing, but the glittering intensity of the summoned-up hallucination* (227).

Perhaps if one were to see the text as an opiate, the question of the reader as mirror might be answered. Now I understand, the reader might say, why the sun seems so extraordinarily bright, why the roses have such an iridescent hue, why the perfume in the air is so pervasive. Why the whole garden has taken on an air of brilliance under the influence of those voices. Those words. But on such trips, as trips go, there is no guarantee the beautiful dream will not turn into a horrible hallucination. I was reminded of the bad acid trip experienced by an acquaintance in my youth. He saw a beautiful sunflower. The sunflower came closer and closer, and he basked in its fragrance until it started to eat him.

In this context, Frye mentions the phrase *ut pictura poesis,* which came ultimately from Horace: *that poetry is a speaking picture, refers primarily to this quality of voluntary fantasy in writing and reading* (227).

The garden as a trope has come to stand for many things. The rose garden could as easily be a magic garden, the lotus leaf of the mind, the couch grass on which one meditates. The garden could be the bower of bliss or the den of errors. It could be the room of one's own. It has not escaped my notice that landscape designers speak of outdoor spaces as if they were indoor spaces. The garden is to be landscaped as if it were a house and divided into rooms. In this context, my rose garden was a room of my own. In Virginia Woolf's essay on that room, she allows for many unspeakable moments of imagination.

One goes into the room, she says, *but the resources of the English language would be much put to the stretch, and whole flights of words would need to wing their way illegitimately into existence before a woman could say what happens when she goes into a room* (91).

Hélène Cixous has echoes in her writing of what Woolf is saying. There is not the language just now to describe the fantasy, the dream, or the hallucination of the woman reading. Instead of being the opportunity to bring the world into being, as Heidegger suggests, language for the woman reading may be a halter. So what goes on in that room is bound to be, as Woolf says, "illegitimate." It may be nearest to simply speak of the secret garden.

You too are in the business of eulogizing love (467), Sören Kierkegaard writes in "The Aesthetic Validity of Marriage," to a "friend." He is defending marriage, perhaps as a kind of garden where human aesthetics may flourish. Yet the spouse as well as the lover are not what they appear to be. All they have done is imitate the true lover: the poet. It is only in verse, in poetry, in poetic language that actual love may be found. *I will not deprive you of what,* he goes on, *indeed, is not yours to own since it belongs to the poet, but of what you have nevertheless appropriated; yet since I, too, have appropriated it, let us be sharers—you get the whole verse, I the last word* (467).

A hierarchy is established: the poet is the source; the philosopher is the perpetrator; the lover is the imitator. In that order.

In light of Kierkegaard's hierarchy, the features of my emotions appeared to me to be sanctioned. It was no longer an aberration that I should prefer the company of my books to that of my lover on certain occasions. Mostly in the mornings, when my papers were spread over the dining table and I was stooped over them, trying to make sense of someone's lost argument. And in the afternoons, when I left all that and retired to the garden. There I could hear birds piping and see butterflies wafting about. There the roses blossomed in red and yellow, and bushes crowded themselves about the stone wall. In that place I had set out to read all of Proust. And at midday, when I went to the campus and did things like sit and chat, photocopy articles, search the library shelves. Daily life had become routine. Only at night, after all that, did I look up and discover something missing.

When it was dark and the streets seemed to close in on the house. But that was also when he would appear, as if by magic. He would be driving off the highway at two hundred miles an hour, spinning wheels at the corner and careening up to my door in his diplomatically immune automobile.

That was after the poetry. And after the philosophy. *And then, too, innocence,* says Kierkegaard (467).

But when these three are all combined: what ecstasy.

On October 25, 1871, George Sand wrote in a letter from Nohant to Gustave Flaubert: Your letters fall on me like a good shower of rain, making all the seeds in the ground start to sprout (248).

On June 4, 1872, Gustave Flaubert wrote in a letter from Croisset to George Sand: *"How much time can I spare you?" Chère maître! But all my time! Now, then, and ever* (274).

But of course, nothing is as it seems.

In April of 1946, Anaïs Nin wrote a surprising entry in her diary: *Writing for me is not an art. There is no separation between my life and my craft, my work. The form of art is the form of art of my life, and my life is the form of the art* (159). She is her own art.

I suspected it was this thought that lay behind the lure of bohemia. The distress that surrounds middle-class life. The ennui of the *Bürgerin*. The shower-curtain syndrome. That you know you have come so far from the source of your feelings. So far from poetry. You have to make restitution to yourself. You have to perform a ritual that will give you back to yourself. That will remove you from the bureaucracy you are in. *I refuse artificial patterns,* Nin goes on. *Stories do not end. A point of view changes every moment. Reality changes. It is relative* (159). You wish to be free to change your mind. To provide no conclusions.

I had been to a reception in Bonn. It was a party in honor of native Canadian culture. Like all such occasions in Germany, there was a great deal of formality. The social hierarchy in the air was thick. As usual on such occasions I went through the affair in a kind of out-of-body way. I was not registering things exactly; only fleeting impressions occurred to me, which I might recollect later at greater peace. Receptions are scatter-brained affairs, and it is hard to talk to ten people at once. I vaguely remember posing for a photograph with a university president and a museum curator. I posed for a photo with Tony Hunt since we were the only two Canadians present. It was not my place just then to correct them. Tony Hunt was reaping the benefits of the unending fascination Germans have for natives of North America. I was feeling absurd. I guessed Tony felt even more absurd. But he was enjoying himself, and I was only appearing to enjoy myself. That was the difference.

At a party in the evening, Tony was the celebrity of the season. It was a garden party. Food was spread on tables on the grass and wine flowed freely. People had congregated not just in the garden, but on all floors of the house. In every room, another intrigue. Eventually, the inevitable happened. Tony was adjured to play his drums and lead an Indian dance. He did. He proceeded to instruct the Germans in the dance. Soon the various guests had covered themselves with blankets and were dancing in a circle.

I looked on with curiosity. This sort of thing could never happen in Canada, could it? Tony was laughing. I think both he and I were as fascinated with the Germans as they were with him.

The party would go on till morning. By the time of the dance, I knew things would get increasingly bizarre. A social orgy would eventually take place. People would be walking around in one another's clothes. They would be paired and tripled up in rooms. I quietly removed myself. I went out the front door and closed the heavy contraption behind me.

I wanted to look at the Rhine River in the moonlight. I found my way to the riverbank by taxi. It was past midnight. The town of Bonn was closed for the night. Streets were empty. I went past the main building of the university and into the adjacent park. There was the water, flowing softly like a silken ribbon. Not as large a river as I always imagined it to be.

The errand I had to the Rhine was private. Something lodged in family memory. Like hundreds of other Scandinavians, my father went to Germany to study. He supported his university career by taking stand-on roles in the German Opera. While the melo-dramatic tragedies of the European imagination acted themselves out hyper-realistically on the German stage, my father stood in the background, holding a spear.

I sat down on a riverside bench. It was at a conjunction of street, park, and river. There was an indeterminacy about the setting. It was hard to tell where one began and the other ended. Facing one way, there was the river. Facing another, there was a street crossing. An empty street. The light of a street lamp shone on the intersection the way the moon shone on the water. So much of northern culture was bound up in that river. Over the centuries, the Rhine has taken on a heavy load of human emotion: tragedy, nostalgia, horror, sentiment. The water was thick with it all. By now, the Rhine was so polluted with the past that it was unsafe for use.

On the other side, the empty street at night

lay there, still wet from an earlier rain. I thought of a comment by Fredric Jameson in *Postmodernism.* In the chapter on "Video," he writes that *The urban street crossing, to begin with, is a kind of degraded space* (92). A place, perhaps, where establishment culture, washing past at my feet, may begin to "come loose from its moorings." To Jameson, the urban street *begins faintly to project the abstraction of an empty stage, a place of the Event, a bounded space in which something may happen and before which one waits in formal anticipation* (92).

For that reason, you find yourself transfixed by the window at night. You are looking at the street. Any moment now, the play may start. It will be a dark production. Sordid, perhaps. Inevitably, *the event fails to materialize and neither of the lovers appears at the rendezvous* (92).

It occurred to me in this summer of reading that the whole idea of "reading" is suspect. We think that to read is to sit down with a book, scan its pages word for word, finish it, and put it away. That is a consumer model of reading, and that is the one we have. Then we make an industry of the commentaries

we produce about the books we have consumed. The
market economy relies on this idea of the reader as
consumer, in order that we may go and purchase
another book, and then another. So we can say "I have
read that book," and it will be equivalent to saying "I
have been to the Andes" or "I have seen India." The
reader as tourist.

But if you care about a book, you will be
"reading" it in a very different way. I have known people to smell their books. A new book, just off the
press, smells glossy, fresh. An old book, taken off a
used bookshop shelf, has the smell of previous readers
on it. The smell of the rooms it has been in. I have
known people to get emotionally involved in the size
and shape of the print, the size of the pages, the color
of the pages and nature of the binding. It is a personal matter. I have known people to carry a book with
them wherever they go. They cannot leave the book
behind: it is too meaningful a possession. There is too
much of themselves in the volume to let it stay
behind. I knew a woman who carried a book of
poems in her purse always. When she felt depressed,
which happened often, she took out the little book
and read a poem for consolation. The book as best
friend. I knew a man who spent his life reading one

work. He spent ten or fifteen minutes every night
before sleep reading a bit of Robert Musil. It was like
a companion through his life, one whom he would
not give up. At least here, he seemed to say, is a soul
mate, an intelligent man on whom I can rely. The
book that holds the world together. People will give a
book to a child or a friend. It is more than a gift: it is
an inspiration. A gesture. The gift of soul, something
that grows with time and does not get used up. This
carrying a book around, this sleeping with a book,
giving a book to another, finding solace in a book:
these are all ways of reading. It is not in a publishing
company's best interests to publish lasting classics. For
such a book will be too satisfying and the reader will
not rush back for another hit immediately.

For me, the summer I spent in Trier was inti-
mately wound up with my reading of Marcel Proust.
In retrospect I can see why. In the three volumes of
Remembrance of Things Past, I had, in fact, a full summer's
reading. There was so much there. I knew the summer
would be confusing and discordant. I knew I would be
treading the minefields of a difficult love relationship.
I knew the work I was doing would be frustrating. I

knew my life would be disrupted socially and emotionally. I would be without family and friends. Without a comforting person to turn to. Proust's narrative would then provide me with a consistency I could string the discordant days on, and it would feel like I had a place from which to measure all other activity.

So I cannot think of my little rose garden without those volumes there. The heavily peopled world of an era gone by. The configurations of a "high society" that no longer existed. The "war" between that society and "bohemians" of the day. The voice that runs through a thousand social situations and holds them in place. Then, this narrative becomes a pool into which other narratives are cast and their reflections are clear.

The relationship, it seemed to me, between writer and reader is reciprocated when the reader is not simply a consumer. At the end of the third volume of *Remembrance*, Marcel Proust, the narrator, has determined that he will now write the book that has, at the point of reading, already been written. He has a fully formed sense of this "book" he will write, which he has been preparing for all his life. He has a clear sense of the reader as well. *It would be inaccurate*, he writes, *even to say I thought of those who would read it as "my" readers. For it seemed to me that they would not be "my" readers but the readers of their own selves, my book being merely a sort of magnifying glass like those which the optician at Combray used to offer his customers* (III:1089).

If the reader can be a mirror, the book may very well be a magnifying glass.

Proust explains: *it would be my book, but with its help I would furnish them with the means of reading what lay inside themselves* (III:1089). The writer does not need to construct a how-to book or a narrative on psychology or sociology or therapy. The writer just needs to write, and the reader, if she is a good reader, will find herself in it. The text will be the land of Oz.

On the writer's side, Proust is not at pains to describe his realizations. Why the writer becomes so involved with the task of writing that all of society fades in importance. He says he sometimes had thought life worth living as he went about in society. But now that he had determined to write his book, it was different. *How much more worth living did it appear to*

me now, now that I seemed to see that this life that we live in half-darkness can be illumined, this life that at every moment we distort can be restored to its true pristine shape, that a life, in short, can be realized within the confines of a book! (III:1088) He has not lived until he has written about his life. *How happy would he be, I thought, the man who had the power to write such a book!* (III:1088) For while you may be happy in your life, your happiness cannot compare with the happiness of the writer who manages to execute his work.

As I sat in the sun, the summer having grown late and the sun a bit lower in the sky, I could see this is only one half of the story. Proust is iterating a classical notion: the elevation of the classical genius. The *Übermensch*, in a sense, for the artist rises above the commonality of human life and renders it all godlike. The artist is able to lend meaning to the life of the reader the way god makes the believer's life meaningful. But this is a romantic idea.

If a woman were to talk about her relationship to her creativity, I wondered, would it be different? What would a woman writer say about this?

Would she be intoxicated with the realization that she had the power to dignify her reader's life? To put a magnifying glass to existence and allow us to see it for what it "really is"? I thought of Anaïs Nin, whose journals are quite articulate on this subject. And in fact, what she says is surprising. In a letter to Leo Lerman, in December of 1946, she writes in response to Lerman's request for a short autobiography: *I see myself and my life each day differently. What can I say?* (198)

The facts lie. I have been Don Quixote, always creating a world of my own. I am all the women in the novels, yet still another not in the novels (198).

It took me more than sixty diary volumes until now to tell about my life. Like Oscar Wilde I put only my art into my work and my genius into my life. My life is not possible to tell. I change every day, change my patterns, my concepts, my interpretations. I am a series of moods and sensations. I play a thousand roles. I weep when I find others play them for me. My real self is unknown. My work is merely an essence of this vast and deep adventure. I create a myth and a legend, a lie, a fairy tale, a magical world, and one that collapses every day and makes me feel like going the way of Virginia Woolf. I have tried to be not neurotic, not romantic, not destructive, but may be all of these disguises (198).

She knows what a chimera a piece of writing may be. What a changeable thing a life is. How subject to fluctuations of mood and temperament. What an illusory thing personal identity can be. How unattainable meaning is. What inaccuracies lurk in every portrait, especially self-portrait.

It is impossible to make my portrait because of my mobility, she writes. (198) *I am not photogenic because of my mobility. Peace, serenity, and integration are unknown to me. My familiar climate is anxiety* (198). No rose garden here. No rest.

I write as I breathe, naturally, flowingly, spontaneously, out of an overflow, not as a substitute for life. I am more interested in human beings than in writing, more interested in lovemaking than in writing, more interested in living than in writing. More interested in becoming a work of art than in creating one. I am more interesting than what I write (198–199).

How text and life become integrated. How one cannot exist without the other. And how does Proust end his great narrative? He is afraid he will have become too weak for the task: that he will have described human beings as though they were giants. *Like giants plunged into the years* (III:1107). The writer as distortionist.

And what does Antonin Artaud say on the subject? *I would like to write a Book which would drive men mad, which would be like an open door leading them where they would never have consented to go, in short, a door that opens onto reality* (59). The arena in which we conduct our lives is not reality. It is a fabrication of our insanities. And even though *all writing is garbage* (85) and all writers are pigs (85), the text is still more real than life.

When I knew I was leaving Germany, and I would not be seeing my lover again for a long time, if ever, I reflected on the haphazard and crazy time we had just spent. Our inconclusive and tense discussions. Evenings in the living room, talking, the lights low, the streets silent. The shutters down. Nights in the cramped bedroom, when I would look over, thinking he was asleep, and I would see his eyes open, staring into the room. The few amicable, if not joyful, hours in Strasbourg. Walking down the street, finding ourselves in the midst of a street parade. Clowns and jesters jumping onto one another's shoulders, yelling at the populace. Stopping every few feet to put on a show. Crowds gathering. Gypsies with beggar bowls and half-naked children.

We would go back to the long-distance phone calls. The hurried visits from him when he could squeeze a few days into his schedule on a mission of diplomacy to North America. The off-hours ringing he would succumb to, when he had too much to drink after a social event for the embassy and came home feeling alone. It was a routine we had become accustomed to. Every morning at nine, my phone rang. For him it was the end of the day. The embassy was closed up for the day and he was the last to leave. My day was just starting. But I knew that after the summer it would not take too long before those communications would grow scarce. No doubt he had seen enough. He could not move me more than this. Such matters are not in our control. He knew that. We both knew that.

He left me at the airport when I went in to catch my plane. I do not remember anything about our parting. I was concerned to get away, to make my date with the airplane.

On the return flight, I happened to be on the same airplane as Tony Hunt, the Haida artist from Vancouver Island who played his drums for the guests at the party in Bonn. When we got to Vancouver, we stopped at the bar and clinked a glass of beer together before heading on. We had a laugh. This Indian was no mere drum player. This was a man of several residences and automobiles, who travelled with his cellular phone, who had offices in Victoria and Qualicum Beach, who was fully technologized and on the Information Superhighway.

Welcome back, we said.

I wanted to leave her, because I knew that by carrying on I should gain nothing (III: 400), says Marcel about Albertine. He finds himself pitched between boredom and pain. The pain of jealousy and the boredom of the bourgeoisie. I thought it is impossible to know what might be gained by staying or leaving. Before he left, on our last night in Frankfurt, my lover looked at me and I saw the uncertainty there. His dark eyes were neither sad nor happy, furious nor relieved. They were all those at once. He just sat and looked at me for a long time. The city quieted down outside the window behind him. The noise of automobiles and airplanes lessened. I was trying to read his face as though it were a book. It had been a good evening. We were close. The tension usually there, an expression I was used to, was gone. I thought of the books I had been reading one last time. My lover's face. A line by Marcel Proust: *If there had been any happiness in it, it could not last"* (III:400).

Sources Cited

Artaud, Antonin. *Antonin Artaud, Selected Writings.* Ed.
Susan Sontag. Transl. Helen Weaver. Los
Angeles: University of California Press, 1988.

Cardinal, Roger. "Toward an Outsider Aesthetic." In
*The Artist Outsider: Creativity and the Boundaries Of
Culture.* Ed. Michael D. Hall and Eugene W.
Metcalf, Jr. London: Smithsonian Institution
Press, 1994. 20–44.

Cixous, Hélène and Catherine Clément. *The Newly Born
Woman.* Transl. Betsy Wing. *Theory and History of
Literature,* Vol. 24. Minneapolis: University of
Minnesota Press, 1986.

Cocteau, Jean. *Diary of an Unknown.* Transl. Jesse
Browner. New York: Paragon House, 1991.

Fish, Stanley. *Doing What Comes Naturally: Change, Rhetoric,
and the Practice of Theory in Literary and Legal Stud-
ies.* London: Duke University Press, 1989.

Frye, Northrop. *The Great Code: The Bible and Literature.*
Toronto: Academic Press Canada, 1983.

Heidegger, Martin. *On the Way to Language.* Transl. Peter
    D. Hertz. San Francisco: Harper Collins, 1982.

Howe, Susan. *My Emily Dickinson.* Berkeley: North
    Atlantic Books, 1985.

Hutcheon, Linda. *Narcissistic Narrative: The Metafictional
    Paradox.* London: Methuen, 1984.

Jameson, Fredric. *Postmodernism, or, The Cultural Logic of
    Late Capitalism.* Durham: Duke University
    Press, 1993.

Kierkegaard, Sören. *Either/Or: A Fragment of Life.* Ed.
    Victor Eremita. Transl. Alastair Hannay. Lon-
    don: Penguin Books, 1992.

Kristeva, Julia. *Black Sun, Depression and Melancholia.*
    Transl. Leon S. Roudiez. New York: Colum-
    bia University Press, 1989.

Kristeva, Julia. *Desire in Language: A Semiotic Approach to
    Literature and Art.* Ed. Leon S. Roudiez. Transl.
    Thomas Gora, Alice Jardine, and Leon S.
    Roudiez. New York: Columbia University
    Press, 1980.

Mariani, Philomena, ed. *Critical Fictions: The Politics of Imaginative Writing.* Dia Center for the Arts, Discussions in Contemporary Culture, Number 7. Seattle: Bay Press, 1991.

Metcalf Jr., Eugene W. "From Domination to Desire: Insiders and Outsider Art." In *The Artist Outsider: Creativity and The Boundaries of Culture.* Ed. Michael D. Hall and Eugene W. Metcalfe, Jr. London: Smithsonian Institution Press, 1994. 212-228.

Nin, Anaïs. *The Journals of Anaïs Nin, 1944–1947.* Vol. 4. Ed. Gunther Stuhlmann. London: Quartet Books, 1979.

Proust, Marcel. "On Reading." Trans. John Sturrock. London: Penguin/Syrens, 1994.

————. *Remembrance of Things Past.* 3 Vols. Transl. C. K. Scott Mocrieff, Terence Kilmartin, and Andreas Mayor. London: Penguin Books, 1989.

Sand, George and Gustave Flaubert. *Flaubert–Sand: The Correspondence.* Transl. Francis Steegmuller and

Barbara Bray. Based on the edition by
Alphonse Jacobs. London: Harper Collins,
1993.

Woolf, Virginia. *A Room of One's Own.* London: Har-
court Brace Jovanovich, 1957.